steep drop

a novel

No Frills
<<<>>>
Buffalo
Buffalo, New York

Printed in the United States of America

White, Kevin Richard

Steep Drop/White- 1st Edition

ISBN: 978-0615755427

1. Steep Drop  – Fiction.   2. New Author – No Frills.  3. Social
Fiction.
1. Title

Cover Design by Frank Masters
Author Photograph by Janelle Heckman

No Frills Buffalo Press
119 Dorchester Buffalo, New York 14213
For More Information Visit Nofrillsbuffalo.com

for bobby,

you saved my life that night out there on the coast.

thank you.

# steep drop

## a novel

by kevin richard white

"Do you really think
that love is gonna save the world
Well, I don't think so
Do you really think
that love is gonna save your soul
Well I sure hope so
I really hope so
But I don't think so"


- The Cardigans, Do You Believe

part

one

I hate breathing air. It's the taste. I don't like how it settles and dies under my tongue or gives up in the back of my throat and I choke on it. I don't like the way it takes up space in my body, the way it flows up and over my nerves or shakes inside of my stomach or puts pressure on my lungs. I don't like the way it kisses my heart. Maybe I'm just paranoid or maybe I just think about things too much, but when I saw her on that day, her eyes staring into me looking for something about me to love again, I've come to accept the fact that air was something I did not need.

What was it that I needed then? I don't know. Things like this never came to me. I always went looking for them. I always went on searches to prove to myself that I could find things if I scavenged long enough. I can't go back and change time – I think that's overrated anyway. I think no one really wants to do that. Well, maybe they do, once in their lives. Maybe when she was staring at me. Maybe that's when I wanted to believe in regret. Maybe that's when I should have taken the deepest breath of my life. I relive it, like an angry movie I created just for the solitary reel in my head.

I'll make the picture up for you. It's cold. Most of these scenes take place in cold weather. We're standing at a park. The playground equipment shivers in the breeze.

The woodchips fly like swallowtails in the vengeful wind. Things become and stay poetic. A lone basketball keeps knocking into the fence, trying to get out. I stand with my hands in my pockets. My hair is short. My throat is dry. My words are twisted. I think of all the things I should have done before I met her. I think of the little things that kill me in the end.

She's beautiful, but I can't tell her that. It's practically an insult now at this point. She'll get tense around her slender shoulders; she'll look off at the highway to count a specific number of cars that drive by before she turns to me and whispers something I can't hear. It's purified combat, this standstill. It gets more and more like a script. I think of my youth, she thinks about growing old. Notice how we'll never strive to reach the same desire – we always squirm away from the marker and try to ignore what it is we really want out of the other. I think of doing something that requires little to no effort, but she thinks of doing something that would take days to do – like bend and recreate a steel structure, or weave a basket, or make a perfect frame for a picture. I would just stare at her. That indifference, that paralysis – that's the cause of these almost-closed eyed glares, the painful, heart-wrenching moments of wrath that make me hate the air I grew up on.

This is certainly the calm, dead afternoon that is waiting to pop like a balloon if you step on the right spot. It's those few hours in the afternoon that just burn – you wish you could laugh, but all you do is just count the seconds you give each other in your slow gazing and you wait until there's a crack in time where you can hop in. But I don't know what else to say about that silence or the cold. I wish I could explain more, but if I did, I have a feeling that I would give up halfway through. It seems bizarre, but if I were ever given a chance to talk my way out of death, I would just take a vow of silence instead. I can't argue if it even would be worth it. It probably wouldn't be. I can't defend myself for too long. I start to get numb. My mouth – again, that air – is taken over by other things and I cannot spit that presence out. I can't bite down on that fine, accumulating mist and remove it with a shake of the head. Rather, I let it build and sugar over, wait until it is deferred, and then I let it explode. Let it trickle out smoothly and start a new puddle for my reflection. The old one is getting blurry.

She, shockingly, moves first. I didn't think she would. She brings her arms closer to her and starts to say something. She wants to shout. She wants to pummel the concrete with her hands, but she is afraid she will hurt herself. She does not like the sight of blood because she is innocent. That's what hurts pretty badly, I think, out of all of this. Even when we gave ourselves the power to jump back and forth, in and out of our domestic shadows, we still don't like the parts that make our whole – our intestines, our valves, our creases, our blood. Maybe it's just the concept of colors that thinly form in the dead spaces we allowed ourselves over the course of a seven year marriage. Maybe we had gotten so old in a matter of a few years that we forgot to tell our bodies to catch up. I don't know. I don't think I ever will. I can't even walk straight anymore and neither can she. She is beautiful but I cannot tell her this. She is so beautiful that I want to die. I want to blind myself with whatever I can find. I'm only saying what I know. I am certain of her skin, her lips at midnight, the exact measurements of her body so my soul can curve along with hers on the rare, fragile moments where we gave ourselves so easily to each other. I am certain that her name is not only a color, but a title – an accurate namesake she can carry with her in her pocket, or in the back of her skull where her words form. Coincidentally, this is the same section of the brain that creates the needles that she is about to say. I am soon going to get stabbed, and I have no other way to let it absorb into me than straight into the face. I blame the air. I blame the begotten wind. I blame the playground equipment.

She still hasn't said anything. I figured I would.

I said her name.

I half expected to be interrupted. But I wasn't. She merely wanted me to stumble over my own rocks, my own uprooted branches to trip over. I am no bomb squad expert nor can I cut away weeds properly. I just step over them and let them build. Which, of course, comes back to get me in the end when I go to clear up my crooked tracks. Her silence hurt me more. I wanted to weep. I wanted to be the poster boy for modern day sympathy.

I tried again, this time, whispering. "I want you to listen." Of course. What else could she really do? It's the one thing she waited for all this time.

"Get to the point." Her words were sharp, like hailstorm rain. Like a hurricane starving for more speed. She always spoke like she was taking care of a small child that was not hers – with extreme love but being aware that it was not all entirely hers. In retrospect, I was her small child. She had loved me and put up with everything that I had ever done solely because she taught her soul to do that without regret or second guessing. But I guess even she understood that even when our marriage began, I was not hers all the way. I was just someone who had wings bigger than she could hold. She could not keep me grounded. But I can't blame her for that. I feel sorry for her. I really do. Because she had made a sacrifice that was to last for eternity, but it blew up in her face like dynamite. I had lit that dream on fire and I had supplied gasoline until my hands were raw. I gained something out of this – it wasn't love from someone else or appreciation from someone else. All I gained out of it was a sense on how to hide – how to create a new face and say new words so your actions won't be linked back to you as quick. What I did not learn was the sense not to do it, but I know, there's payback to be involved. She would be the one to unload her fury on me. I was her paper-thin target practice sheet, hanging naked on a steel pole. She had unlimited time to make me suffer.

I tried to search in vain for a point. It's easier to confess these things to you because you will not judge me or hold me in front of a jury. You won't cast me aside and you won't call me over for dinner later. You're a transparent stranger under the employ of a spiritual motivation to listen to all of this and make an opinion, and when your time is up or when my time is up, you will move on and create a new section of your life where you take this story, keep the elements you love, throw the other bits and pieces over the edge to die, and you will tell someone else this. Someone you love and trust. Your point is to keep this going because we know that human passion overrides all else in the long run. Her point is to know the truth. My point is broken, short-changed, immature and stillborn – my point died the very minute I decided to give myself to another place that did not have her. Caskets have been created for all of us – her, me, you. But now, I place my foot in that casket. The two of you will live because you love being sacred. I, like many others, chose the other path. Not because I wanted to see what was down there, but because I am permanently slanted. There's no cause to straighten me out. There's no attempt to be made by you or anyone else to change how I am because I'm not even sure how to do that myself.

I have many sins, but until I either burn them off my body or laugh them out of my system, they'll stay with me, biting, until I either give into them or call them something else and pretend that they're a gift.

She smiles suddenly. I turn and I see that one of her favorite cars drive past. I always forget the name of it. But, brief as it was, the happiness subsides. As it makes a sharp left onto a side street, her smile dies as quick as it was created. It must be so wonderful to erase emotions at will. I'm very jealous of her when it comes to that, how can she pretend, even if for a flashing second, to be happy when clearly she isn't. I wish I could easily change my face like other people can. But the crow's feet, laugh lines and wrinkles stay on me. Instead of a youthful smile, I have pity. I have envy where my light blue eyes should me. I contain afterthoughts instead of bright, white teeth. I have, right by my jaw line, a never-ending desire to apologize for the horrible things I've thought and done. I haven't told you the whole story, of course. But you'll listen because you're interested and because I'm not done talking.

"I don't have a point," I finally say. I take a step closer, but she doesn't move. I'm thinking this is progress.

"I do," she bitterly shouts at me. She crosses and re-crosses her arms for security and comfort. She has skinny arms, but very pale white skin that I love so much. They're strong arms. They're arms that held me when I've hit the wall, the floor, fell down the steps, tripped going up steps and even in places where I never thought I'd be held – parking lots, bookstores, ice cream shops. They're arms that I'll welcome even if I was stone. But I'm not totally human anymore, so I can't enjoy them. I'm a virus. I'm deceit. I'm sadness. She is fragile – the softest, weakest form of glass that cannot hold anything heavy – and if she were to hold me down, my pain would drop right through her pane and frame and clatter and spread all over the floor, both me and her. So all we do is stand and point fingers in the middle of this park. If we're sleeping, we're content. But when we're awake, we're broken. It's a riddle from some horrible dream. She goes to add something else, but she cannot. Even when she is like this, a shadow that I don't fully understand, she is beautiful. I love her, and because I love her so much, I can't allow anyone else to love her, even you. I could be married to someone else, or seeing someone else years down the road, and if she were looking for someone to love her back, I would make her only love me, solely because I love her to the point where I can't even stand straight. I know that makes no sense. But to me, it does. It only makes sense to me and for that, I guess I'm glad. It makes me breathe a little easier. I don't have to wage so much war anymore.

"You ignored me. You disappeared. Explain that," She says. I admire that she is not drowning in tears yet. Her muscles shake and she looks like death yet I'm fully taken aback by her determination not to let go of her emotions. She is definitely stronger. It's her heart. Her family has had strong hearts and hers is no different. I've heard it talk – nights I lazily lie on her chest but never let myself sleep. It thumps delicately, gently – as if it were rain pouring through ripped plastic bags. That's what holds her together. At times where I was mad at the world,

I'd go to it like a drug. These are things I cannot tell her. I fear that she will think I'm silly or that the feelings will not be reciprocal. And now I know that love is now the ultimate fraction, at least ours, and there is no such thing as reciprocal. They are fragmented numbers, hanging on something very small.

"I can't explain that."

"You have to."

"There's no excuse."

"We're talking in circles. Get to the point or I'm leaving."

"Please don't leave."

She wants to spew fire, but she is timid. She wants to reach deep down into herself and pull out some sort of ammo that will wipe me dead and clean off of this world. She wants to take back every kiss and add it up and throw it back into my face with enough force that it will make me go blind. She wants to stomp and choke me until I die in this cold park, alone and with a shattered throat. But she cannot. And I couldn't do it to her if I were in her shoes. I don't think death is an end. It's just more of what we have now. It's only intensified. It's gold that doesn't shine; it's the part of the balance beam where you always watch people lose their footing and fall. It is life only exploded to the point where you cannot piece them back together.

The grief stays. The mortality becomes a joke. She wants to ruin my life, but she cannot because I ruined hers first. She can never get me back because she has lost her spine, her ability to stop pressure building in her head. She is the victim of a gigantic loss. Because of me. I broke her legs, her wings. She senses that I'm narrating to you about her so she walks toward me and stops maybe two steps away. Our faces become mirrors. She reads my mind sometimes. That's something I'll never find in anyone else, ever again. Whether or not it'll keep me up at night, whether it'll make me cry when I'm alone, I'll know in due time. But at this moment, I don't understand anything. Just her beauty. Just her being.

"Why did you forget who I was?"

She goes for a tough question. "I don't know what you mean."

She continues to stare deep into me. I feel uneasy but calm at the same time. I want her to take this horrible air out of me. But she won't. She'll let me suffer. Lovers do it, they do it well, and they always and forever will.

"You completely vanished. Do you know how scared I was?" She's about to cry. Right now, I'm starting to feel it. I start to get drunk on the pain. I finally know, I think, what it's like to abandon your safety, leave your comfort zone and destroy others along the way. I don't need a dictionary right now to fully define hurt. I have it memorized and saved for whenever I need it. I'm ashamed. I'm ready to vanish again, this time as a vapor, to slink back into molecules where her hands cannot touch me. I don't deserve her. She deserves better. But I cannot let her go because I love her, and she cannot let me go because she wants answers I cannot give. We have learned different languages in our time apart. We need a translator. But all of those are dead.

"I think I do."

"You don't. I don't think you ever will. I wanted to die."

"Don't say that." She can say whatever she wants, she's a grown adult. But she can't say that. I won't let her.

"I can say whatever I want to say. You owe me that much."

She's right. There's nothing I can hold her back on. She needs to vent. I put my hands in my pockets. I wanted to give them to her as a way of apologizing, but she would smack them away. I feel helpless. We're standing at a place where kids play and we're arguing instead. It's an unfortunate sight for those who want to be happy and we're being the complete opposite. We're orbiting around the idea of staying together: we're floating in a dead space instead of a universe meant for peace. I'm just glad no one is watching. If someone is, from their windows, I'm sure they're enjoying the surrealism of it all. I hope they're recording it, because I know three or four days from now, I'm going to want to retrace my steps.

Her hair was blowing in the cold wind. Of course it was, it's impossible for it to do anything else. In my mind, I know I shouldn't be saying these things, but I want to remember all of this. And hopefully, the flash that runs through our eyes before we die will contain all of this. I don't want to remember being old and alone. I just want to remember being young and seeing her. Our faces were starting to become so numb that I wanted to take my hand and let it become alive again. But I keep forgetting that actions like that is not my purpose anymore. My one job is to now stand and listen as she rips me open and replaces it with whatever else she finds. I'm not her domestic shield anymore. I'm her torn blanket she clutches with frenzy. I'm not shying away from this new responsibility. It's who I am now. I can't change it.

"Go ahead."

"No. You talk. Why did you go away without saying one fucking thing to me for three years?"

So now you know. She had said it before I could. I did leave. I left for three years, two months and fourteen days. I left on a Wednesday, shortly before dinner, as she was taking a nap and I couldn't sleep. So I left. It remains a blur, and it will never level out, but that is the easiest I can say it without stopping myself. I ignored her for that long – every phone call, every letter, every chance I drove back to this town to see my parents or friends – and I was in fear every minute of that period of my life. I was in shaking, trembling fear. I left love at home for the unknown. She was the best woman I could have ever asked for. Yet I left her. And until I die, I have to live with that. I left soft hands, quiet nights reading, hiking, kissing, and midnight moments sitting on the balcony watching breathing snow fall past our bodies and onto the ground to build and keep warm. I had noticed more beauty in my time with her that I had when I was dreaming – yet I made the decision to disappear. I had shed my identity and I left her in the cloud of dust. I ravaged her, I annihilated her, and I watched in daydream as she took her wedding ring off and smashed it with a hammer I left behind. I do not blame her one second for anything. I love her. But that is the truth. I left her alone to die on her own, to live and sleep and eat on her own, to watch movies on her own, to work on her own, and to listen to what it might be like for my new life without her completely and utterly on her own, with her soul crying at every second. I'm very sure the sound of her bones breaking, her skin cracking, and her hair falling out, her eyes closing kept her awake for three years where she forgot the meanings of all the words I've mentioned to her. She had learned to evolve without me. But now, like lovers always are, we still stand here to play one last guessing game. We haven't changed. If we're separated, we have. But together, we still pause at the same moments whenever we confess.

"I was afraid."

She stared at me like I was fading. I half expected her to grab me and look at me in her hands like I was some forgotten element. I thought of her innocence and how I crushed it.

"You were afraid?"

I nodded.

"You disappeared for three years and you didn't tell me why because…you were afraid."

I kept nodding. I couldn't look at her for this part. I'm a coward.

A lot of time passed before she said, "I hate you."

"I know you do."

"You don't know how much."

I believed her. It didn't take her long to come to her conclusion, but it still stung.

"I hate you so fucking much right now. I want to see you dead." She whispered the second half to make me listen.

"No, you don't."

"Yes, I do." Then, she couldn't hold it in anymore. She started to cry. Not heavy sobbing, but two suicidal tears ran down her cheeks and fell onto a pile of leaves at our feet. I had shot down everything she ever had faith in. I wanted to take the tears away with my thumb, but if I did, the hate would be amplified. She would not want me touching her right now, even if she had begun to lose all of her body at once. She would rather me watch as she lost consciousness and her limbs at the same time.

After a long pause, I said, "I guess you have every right to."

"Think about what you did!" She suddenly spat out with anger, almost cutting me off. "Do you think that you would be forgiven? Why don't you be a fucking man?"

My only response to this is I don't know how to be. I don't know who that man is. I certainly don't know the person that's telling you this right now. I'm just telling you because I experienced it.

I started to say her name.

"Don't say my name."

"Fine."

I can't say her name to you because I will die. I will kill myself before the story ends if I said her name to you. So I can't. Just fill it in with whatever you feel is necessary. Whatever sounds right. And I won't tell you mine because I'm sure you may know somebody with the same name, and that's disrespect to them. Because I'm sure all of them have more honor and balls than I ever will. We are nameless. That'll stay that way for the rest of eternity.

We stood there in silence a few moments before she took a few steps back and turned her back on me. She looked out onto the park. Swaying trees were our audience, as was a little stream underneath a crumbling stone bridge, the aforementioned playground equipment only there for what seemed to be ghosts instead of actual children, the basketball courts, the roads, the future. The past and the present. The sheer undeniable horror that at four in the morning I will revisit this place exactly how I came into it: no color, no hope, no exit. The panic that she will be just bones and a rambling mouth with nothing for me to grab on to as my dream recognizes my sins and punctures me over and over until I simultaneously die from blood loss and wake up. I will play this movie again and again until I memorize my lines and then naturally ask for a script change. I'm left to revolve around these possibilities in my head and being sober or drunk won't help fix the problem. This standstill is eternal and available in all moods. I will have to go back into the apartment someday with her following me, screaming, as I get back the few possessions I hope she didn't get the courage to throw away. I'm guessing they're not there, but maybe they are as a sign of her being hopeful that I would return from the journey unscarred and unaware of how long I was really gone. But again, I'm hoping too much. I expected the caring side of her, like an idiot. The one that I had gotten shown up with the intent to kill. I thought she had turned around to walk away, but instead she stood there, shivering. She was still crying. I walked up next to her. So close to putting my arm around her. Maybe that's what she wanted. To see that I still had feelings for her. Eventually, I did.

She did not move.

I studied the shapes of the trees in silence. I let the wind in its waves bump into me and not apologize afterwards. The skin of my body seemed to wrap itself with wire as it braced itself deeper and deeper with every blast of cold. I studied senses for so long that it was almost as if I had invented them. I looked back at her and I realized I shouldn't say anything; language was so crazy, so frantic, that if I somehow blurted what I was really feeling, it would interrupt her calm bloodstream, her rapidly growing appreciation for an almost elusive quiet. I thought of faith suddenly as I would of a basket: one that needed weaving, careful measurement, a watchful eye to see over it, and a steady hand to craft its core so that you could carry it and let it not be empty, let it not have holes, let it not be crooked or ready to spill its contents. I realized that the search would be like a cross that you would have somewhere in your life: in your car, your pocket, your messenger bag. I didn't even reach for her hand. I didn't have to. I knew how it felt. I knew what it had inside. It had something that I could never explain. It almost felt like a beginning despite the end we were so closed to having just then. Over the years, I gave birth to many things: fading glances, burning gazes, static, among other things that carried a horrible weight; but I decided that, while I was here standing still and freezing to death, that pain was just weakness, a bag that had no handle. It was time to shed that child and create something nobler in return.

But again, she would not understand this. Me standing there was the closest she would get to understanding it. All of this will have to stay with you.

Whatever you chose to do with it is up to you, but just keep it with you for a while.

She said my name, like it was a piece of prayer.

Her soft voice finally ruined this peace and quiet. I was grateful for the death of that.

"I don't know what to tell you. I really don't. I just…I left because I needed a break. A breath of fresh air. I was tired. Very tired," I said.

"I don't know if that works…"

"It's the truth. I don't know what it was about staying here, but I just couldn't do it. I had to move on. I had to get over you."

She looked at me. She looked at me for a long time before I finally said:

"But of course, I'm not."

For the first time that day, she finally smiled. It almost crushed my heart. It had made me so happy to see that. For once, I made her satisfied. I didn't know whether it was luck or what, but something urged me to keep going.

"I was stupid to leave. I couldn't tell you this because I was afraid that you had wanted to stay here and let things just be normal and ordinary. I was afraid that you had just wanted to be…this forever."

"I don't believe you," she finally whispered.

"But you have to. This is the closest I can get…"

"I don't think I ever will. Or could. We really are talking in circles. We honestly are. We're getting nowhere. I'm leaving."

"Then why the fuck did you just smile at me?"

"I don't know. Just don't follow me. It was stupid for me to come out here. I should have just let myself believe that you were dead. It would have been better that way. Maybe for all of us."

She broke away from me and started to walk very fast back to her car. It was one that she must have bought very cheap after I left – parts were barely hanging on and the paint was chipped. It probably sounded like death when she drove it, but she didn't care, because it became a form of expression for her – something that accurately described her feelings because nothing else would. I saw her body go farther away from me. I got to the sudden realization that if I not make one more chance to stop her, I would never see beauty again. I would have dust in my eyes forever. I couldn't live with being blind. I had to go for it. I needed her. I would rather have her not understand me than walk away from me.

I screamed.

She ignored me.

I screamed louder.

I thought of when we had first met. You never forget that moment. You may forget what lead up to it, but when it all comes together and you're able to lock eyes for the first time and you see what the other person is made up of, and you begin to talk, you never forget that. You store it away somewhere. With her, it became a library. I had built a shelf just for her and I can go back to it whenever I choose. I have her moments alphabetized, her fears categorized, all of her dreams and wishes and loves and hates gathered in one book with solid binding so it never rips or tears or bursts at the seams. It stays in an easy place that even if someday I get a broken arm or can't walk I can still get to it and read it. In this book I know everything about her. But what I didn't know was right now. I was never going to know how this was going to go. I was prepared for her to be mad, to leave, to walk out and wish me dead – but I didn't want to happen. I didn't know this chapter. I was mad. I was frustrated and I wished suddenly for someone else to come in and just be a mediator. In a moment of panic, I picked up a rock. I threw it. I didn't want to hit her. I just wanted to get her attention. But it hit her in the back of her leg and she whirled around. Even from far away, I knew her eyes caught on fire. I was going to get hit back finally.

"What the fuck is your problem?"

"This doesn't have to end like this."

"Why did you hit me?"

I ignored her and said it louder. "This doesn't have to end like this! It doesn't! Don't walk away and get back here. I'm not talking to you." Ironic – I didn't even know what to say.

"Don't give me orders."

"Don't walk away."

"I'll do whatever the fuck I want. And if you hit me again, I'm going to kick the shit out of you."

"I didn't mean to. I tried to hit your car. Or the ground. I don't know." I felt like I've just been caught doing something bad in elementary school. I became really embarrassed.

"I can't believe you would even try to do something like that."

"Don't leave. It really doesn't have to end this way."

"I think it does. You told me nothing about what happened. You just left me. I don't want to live like this. I'm better off without you."

"Give me another chance."

"What is with you and giving? Give me this, give me that. After you took everything away from me, from us, and from yourself. Don't give me that. I let you come here and say your piece, and of course it wasn't anything worth listening to." She stopped for a minute to rub her leg on the spot where I hit her with the rock. I wanted to touch those legs again. I wanted to do the things that I once considered naughty but now consider essential to love. I felt dirty and sacrilegious, but I thought that if I did it again, maybe I would be saved. It's wrong of me to think of sex when we're at the reconciliation part, but I suppose that goes to show how fucked up I am. I thought she was going to continue, but instead, I picked up another rock. I really don't know why. I held it out like I was going to give it to her. I don't know why I did that either. Part of me – well, really all of me – was paralyzed. Yet I was moving. No one ever really knows how we can still do these things when our heart is pounding.

"You going to hit me again?"

"No. I just…"

"You what?"

I felt like I was fighting an army. I gripped it tighter. "I love you. And I don't know how else to tell you or show you."

"Leave me alone. You try to hit me again…and I will hit you back."

"I didn't try to hit you! Jesus. I told you that."

"Put it down."

I looked at it like it was the softest thing on Earth. I didn't want to let go of it. It was bringing more comfort than anything else at the moment.

"Drop it, now," she said.

But before I could, she walked up to me and grabbed me – hard – at the wrist. I dropped it, but I guess I got mad that she grabbed me so hard that I went to grab her wrist. She moved away and tightened her grip on me so I couldn't hit her. But, suddenly, I decided to kneel down and drag her. Her body went with mine on the ground and we both fell in the dirt. She was on top of me and dug her nails into my flesh. I screamed and tried to push her away, but my hands wound up on her breasts and she took that as an advance, I guess, so she started to claw into my eyes. I grabbed her wrists and pushed her back and then brought her down onto the grass. I could feel blood – and then see it – trickle down into her face and her shirt. Her nice clothes, now ruined. It started to drip into her mouth as she was screaming, and she dug her nails into any spot of mine she could reach. I started to scream at her and she started to scream back, but before I could stop myself and see what I was truly doing to her, she kneed me in the groin, and then as I let go, she slapped me in the face. I fell back, she stood up and took her now bloody palm across my shirt, staining it, and letting me wear my own blood. Her face, speckled with red spots, was now just about on fire, and in pain, more pain that I knew that she never felt before.

"You fucking attacked me."

"No, I did not."

"I don't want to sit here and be a fucking child with you anymore! You attacked me!"

"No, I didn't! Jesus Christ. You fucking clawed into me. Look!" I wiped blood off my face and showed her. "You did this to me."

"Goddamn it, I didn't want to be this kind of person. Ever. But you did this, you goddamn prick. You made me like this."

"You made this like this! Fuck, babe. Why did you have to dig into me like that?"

"You deserved it, you bastard. And don't call me babe. You don't have the right to call me shit like that."

I tried to sit up. The pain was too much so I sat there in the grass. I saw the rock I wanted to throw and it again became something that meant nothing to me. So I stood there and watched her. Her nails bore my flesh. She wanted to mark me again. But not as hers. She just wanted to mark me so everyone else would know something hidden about me.

"Don't come near me," she finally said.

"Just give me more time to talk."

"Why should I? Why should I give you reason to do anything?"

"Because isn't this what you wanted?"

"What, your bullshit? No, what I wanted from you was to stay with me and be with me. You married me for a reason. I don't think leaving was the right way to go about it."

"Well, of course not, but…"

"But what? Tell me. Do you have an answer for that?"

Eventually, I think I would. But not for a very long time. I've had a bad history on searching for things like that. Today probably wouldn't be a good day for it either.

"Do you have an answer for anything? I mean, honestly? Do you have an answer for your childhood, or our teenage years, or our marriage, or anything sacred? Is there something that I could have done better? Is it something about me that is so out of your league that you had to just go? How lost was I that you decided that I couldn't be found? And the kid? You wanted to do this with the kid and you wanted a family with me and then you just left and then I don't know…I don't know what to think or where to go or what to say. You wanted a kid and then all of a sudden..." Her tears ended the argument quietly. She dots her eyes with her knuckles, looking at all the blood that she spilled, and with a quick hair flip, her sights are back at me, in the cold and the anger.

"I knew you wouldn't," she whispered soon after. She turned away again.

"Stop," I said, finally managing to stand up. The blood, I'm sure, was running down my face faster than I felt it. I looked down at my shirt and saw it smiling red back up at me.

"No. This is over. Go back to where you came from. Go back to fucking hell."

"Give me some more time..."

"Go back to wherever you called home. Because it wasn't with me."

"You're where home is."

"Bullshit."

"Just listen...quit yelling and just listen, please."

"Listen to me. You need to listen to me now. I gave you a chance and you fucking blew it. After three years, all you had to say was that you needed a change of scenery and you loved me but decided I wasn't good enough to go with you. That's weak. That's really fucking weak. Everything that you ever said to me now means absolutely nothing. So now let me tell you what I decided after three quiet, depressing years."

I was never more scared in my life to hear this.

I wanted to daydream more than anything, but at that point, I could not. I just wanted this to be over. I wanted her to stab me, to push me into space.

I thought she was going to speak. I thought I was going to die. I thought of whirlwinds to carry me away, but nothing could stop her. She was in motion, beginning to walk towards me.

I thought for a minute I did die.

She came up to me and stopped so close to me that our eyelashes almost touched. I looked straight into her eyes and I just saw flame. But a quiet flame – one that might be put out if you just put the fire between your fingers and lightly pressed the prints together. It had no color, it had no consistency or anything. In her eyes I saw and felt passed time. I saw abandonment, I had seen children's stories that had been left behind at the shelves of bookstores, crossed out children's names, expired honeymoon plans, dinner plates still clean. She turned her gaze down at my lips. I never had thought about her lips this whole time. I thought about what I could do them if she knew I was being completely sincere. I felt like I could gain her back. I saw her body now with my blood on it and I felt excitement, that she had my fluids on her again, that she saw my insides and felt them, on her skin, beneath her fingernails, in the quiet dirt. I wanted to become both a bandage and scar. And I saw it through her eyes, her lips. Her entire existence.

She put her soft hand on my cheek. The nails lightly grazed beneath my eye and I felt their chipped roughness cut me to some extent. I would welcome more hurt to wake me up from this nightmare. I realized now that dreaming was not going to get me away from her. It was only going to bring me closer. It was only going to drag me back to a moment like this, where our skin is forced to touch again, where our eyes are only centimeters away from seeing into those closed windows, where anything and everything else falls by the wayside so I can prop myself back up again and become that support for her. I felt the skin of her palm. I felt like I was home. I felt I had learned reincarnation and I was lucky enough to wind up in the same body as my own one hundred years later after some hasty, quick demise. I felt like my whole life had waited for this – for me to go, for me to come back, for me to rediscover and reach.

Her lips came towards mine. I wanted them. Mine opened. My eyes closed. We were so close.

But she closed hers.

She drew a sharp, quick breath.

I opened my eyes.

She gave a humorless smirk and blew her breath into my mouth. She took the palm that was on my face and with all her force pushed me down onto the ground. My shoulder hit a sharp group of rocks and I got a mouthful of dirt. I whirled around to where I could see her, still standing there, acting as if she was still going to kiss me.

"That's what it fucking feels like. That's what I've decided. Get the hell out of my life. Wherever you went, just stay there. You're not wanted here. By anyone."

I stayed silent. I had nothing to say. I just sat on the ground, feeling the warmth from her body come so close to mine. I felt like I was going to be cured.

I watched as she gave me one last hard stare from her beautiful eyes. I felt, again and certainly not for the last time, real pain. She got into her car. She did what she had to do. I watched her drive away as it began to snow on the most destroyed man on the planet. I counted the snowflakes as they finally came as promised. She disappeared, like a lover's final line in some story. She came and went like water through a fire, like a kiss between drifting people. She had gone. She had left me.

And she with a place to go, and with possibly someone to hold her as she cried and washed off my blood.

I had none of that. I only had one place other to go.

My legacy of life is simply this: I'm in love with a woman who does not love me back and I can't even tell where home is. I don't miss home because I have none and because of that, it is not missing me back. It is a sad, retarded, fucked up love affair, and it's so stereotypical that it makes me want to laugh, weep, break my hands all at once. I'm only driving because it's been engrained into me. It's habit. It's a cynical way of escaping what bothers me, it's a mediation technique where I pretend I'm normal and when I lie to others and say I don't have stress when clearly it eats away at me.

It seems like I'm driving without glass. The mirror is so clear and the softness of its pain lingers, as snow falls and pelts the pane, stains with its moisture, almost like blood, and calmly I wipe away the remains and cast them to the side of the road where they will dance and huddle with cold, bent leaves. The broken, crumbled spines of the leaves also hit the windshield, and again, I wipe them away, saying my goodbyes as the words never seem to come out: they limp around in the curves of my mouth, never getting past the lip, and out to a spot where sound can carry it the rest of the way. My voice, in the beauty of tonight, is poison. I make a hairpin turn onto a quiet side road where sticks and stones lay on the concrete like gold in a pan after you sift out the dirt. They shine and smile. I'm thinking again and again in fragments that don't fit together – it's like I got ten thousand different sheets of paper and I cut them up in some insomniac frenzy, and now, I can't find where they join back up again. It's weird – my heart is dying, I'm driving with no rhyme or reason, and I'm noticing all of these things around me, giving them attention, instead of myself. Sometimes I can be really selfless, but you know by now that I'm not really reliable or a nice guy. I blame so many things. I can't name them all. Right now, I'm just letting the movie continue on. This is obviously the beautiful intermission that no one notices because everyone left the theatre. Except me. I notice the shattered leaves, the snow, and the sound of my car passing through this night.

My tires go over them in a matter of half-seconds and I liken the sound to bones being crushed: maybe not crushed, but rebuilt, to become beautiful again in another universe, after I go through this one and a new one starts after I go onto another road. I'm drunk with thought. I'm smiling; despite the cold. My cheek is warm, only being minutes after you touched it. I felt everything about you. I started to daydream of a world that I thought was going to exist mere minutes before I saw you. You had crashed those hopes, but I'm going back to it because it still makes me happy.

In your eyes, you looked at my hands: measured the veins, the decaying skin around the nails, the flat knuckles, and the vise-like grip I have when I'm holding something that makes me angry. Softly, you take my fingers and interlock them with mine. The voice behind that is enough to make me stagger off and recount my blessings. It's enough to infect bad memory and kill it dead. I can see you glistening in the snow. Quietly dancing, surprised you're moving so fluidly, with calm, cautious, careful steps, your short hair sparkles with light wet flakes that drip in odd time signatures back to the ground where it meets its friends again. You don't care about damp feet or lack of sleep. You just whisper for me to come there, and I imagine myself getting out of the car and stepping through the clear glass, and taking you at the elbow. There's a spot of your elbow I like to hold the most. It makes you flinch a little, but otherwise, I believe you love it just as much as I do. But I don't dance and you don't make me. We stand and hug each other. I smell all of your smells and you grab onto me like a ladder leading somewhere nice. I feel your palm latch onto my body as if it's the only thing that will stabilize you. You use me for balance in the cold. You use me for warmth, both in words and in actions.

I end the daydream out of fear that I will wreck the car. I keep driving. I love you, I say out loud. The steering wheel does not respond. The radio, humming, does not respond. I say it again. The snow committing suicide on the glass does not respond. Nor does the road or the trees, the swaying branches that shiver from the frozen air, or the box of tools in my backseat. My hands clench the rubber. I say it one more time, as a gentle song to myself, one that will float around me like a dream until I lay my head down to sleep. That's when you'll say it back. That's the only moment when you'll say it back - when I'm closing my eyes and I feel your heat in my head, when I see you, when I'm just about to join you again in a place where I don't let in anyone else but you and the silence.

I think of her like this. I feel like you should know. Even though I made an exit from her life and that I don't deserve her, I still hold her in such high regard that it both makes me proud and sickens me. I place her in these errant situations where recklessness could lead to her not appearing in anymore of them, but I know that I can take care of her still, in moments where my emotions seem to be dangling over the ledge. Even though that I might be insane, I still keep my priorities in a safe room away from anything else – even if space is running out and the calmness of it is running super thin. I think she requires something akin to perfection – I know that perfection is a myth and those who think it is true and real are just fooling themselves. I guess I can say this because I tried to fight for it for so many years and I wound up getting a thinly veiled version of the real thing. It wasn't something I could really show anyone. It wasn't something I could tell anyone. Perfection just became something you only read about in stories that are too good to be true – and if the world needed someone to fuck up their life to figure that out and tell others, then I am kind of glad it was me in the end, because I'm honestly a lot happier now knowing that what I spent so many years fighting for is just nothing. I need to tell others this, which is why you're here. You're here so you can learn from my mistakes, so you can be more appreciative of life. So that when you're older and in my position, you can notice all the things I'm doing and all the mistakes I'm doing and work around that and make better decisions. I like to think I'm doing a service. But I'm just hurting everyone in the process. I'm hurting her, I'm hurting myself, I'm hurting all of my friends who are no longer my friends. They have every right to hold a grudge like they do and I don't blame them. But I just want them to put their hatred aside long enough just so they can read this and hopefully they'll get the vibe that for once, I actually mean what I say and that I'm not just joking about anything anymore. If there is a big joke, it's just me. I want them to understand that.

I come to a four way intersection and stop. I feel like my face is on fire – I wipe my face with my hand and I find tears. I haven't even noticed. My lips still sting from her move. I can't be mad at her. I can only accept. I can't judge her. She can only judge me. I just wanted it to be real so badly. A storybook ending. Man jilts woman, begs for forgiveness, gets her back. But now I realize how fucked up I truly am because no story I have ever read actually ends with that happening. So I guess I'm an eternal optimist with a penchant for bad luck. It happens. But sadly far too often.

I'm waiting far longer than I should at this intersection because I realize I can't see in front of me. The roads are drowning in fog. Silver pockets of tightly woven air are preventing me to go back to nowhere. Maybe it's for the best. I look behind me to see if anyone is coming up in the rearview mirror – they're not. Afternoon quickly transformed into night and I suppose that the snow is keeping everyone away from me. I'm ok with that, though, they're together as one, and I'm simply not meant to be. I can accept that too. I reverse the car and pull into a little field all by itself. I drive the car into the fog to the point where I know for sure I'm away from the road. I let the engine die. I have turn off the heat as well and maybe it's better for a while if I just take away the things that are supposed to make me feel better so I can suffer greater.

I could tell you story after story about how her and I were in the beginning. But I don't know how exciting or memorable that would be for you. I'm sure it's almost like every other "young couple in love" story that you heard before. I could tell you what we did and how much time we spent and how we felt like we were younger than we really were, but I feel like if I go back to that enough times, the memory will wear thin and it will cease to exist. Then I would have nothing to go back to. I wouldn't have a fallback dream to go to whenever I felt horrible. I couldn't stop thinking of her lips. How they were so close to my body. How time stood still. Her hands, even. How soft they were. How they touched me. How I thought I was going to avoid dying or getting hurt and that somehow, she would let me pass out into her arms and she would carry me back to our house and we could start over. I thought for sure she would have looked different. I thought maybe she would have cut her hair or started wearing different clothes, or gained weight, or lost weight, or maybe tried some new form of walking or something, but she was exactly the same way I left her. I can't tell you how happy I am for that, at least. That despite all of what happened, she never changed physically. But how mistaken was I that in the time that was lost between us, she went from a saint to a snake – something with bite, and something that did not walk, but simply vanished as quickly as she came.

I take my cell phone out of my pocket – currently, the last connection I have to getting in contact with her. I want to call her so bad. I feel like it's a horrible idea if I do, but at this rate, I almost have no options left. I'm a weak person. I have no energy to go to therapy and have someone analyze me. I have no energy whatsoever to go to bed or to sleep or to rationalize my decisions. I'm just doing them just to do them. I guess in some weird cosmic way, I'm living my life the way I choose to and I'm just writing down every mistake I make along the way, so that when I die, no one has to ever wonder about anything I ever did at any point in time. It makes the chronology a lot easier to maintain. There are specific points that we can go back and revisit. Like the visit with her. And now, the episode in my car. The world keeps turning. Camera film keeps being used. My eyes close an infinite number of times and reopen an infinite amount of times and I still become disappointed with what I don't find when I open them back up to reality. But I suppose if reality and fantasy were the same thing, we would have all died when we were five years old, trying to learn how to fly.

As I'm staring at the phone, debating what to do with it, thinking of the voice and girl on the other end of it, I'm forcing myself to fall back on a memory I thought I had properly forgotten. But they're children. And they stay. And they cling on. I'm thinking now of a time where I had saved her from a situation that she may not have want to be saved from. It's so stupid now because at the time, I was actually being heroic, romantic and a real person. I look back on it and I think I could have handled it so differently, and I'm not necessarily proud of it, but I don't have much to be proud of. It all started when:

*One night, when we were much younger, actually - when we first got married. Maybe eight or nine months after we got married. We're struggling for money. I hadn't taken her out to dinner in a long time, maybe even since we started dating. I just can't remember these things anymore. I'm sure she would be able to tell you if you asked her. But I do remember we were poor, dirt poor.*

*Our jobs were just words. They were not careers, they were nearly flickering moments that we couldn't grab or cherish. But we were trying to use our youth, not waste it. Anyway, whatever you want to call it, her and I had dinner had some place I can't even remember, and afterwards, we went out to this bar. I remember going to it several times before, but it was at a time where I wasn't too proud of my drinking, and I didn't want her to know I ever had a problem. This was years before I met her, but those past demons come up unconsciously and rather quickly, and I had to bite down on the memories of the place before I spilled them out to her. She seemed to be having a good time, and we really hadn't planned on having a lot - just a few long enough to prolong this night as something worthwhile. But time had been as fickle as each other, and we were well into the night that we were both safely drunk and not ok to go anywhere else but the bathroom.*

*She said my name about after the fifth one.*
*"What?"*

*She smiled at me, toyed with my belt. Her eyes were dancing wildly. A plague of love was running through her. For once, she had not one worry on her face. And she was almost gorgeous enough to keep. Later did I realize how deep that face was rooted into my life, how* powerful the connection was between my love of that regard.

"Let's fuck," she whispered.

"Where?"

"I don't care. Anywhere."

"We're in a bar. And we're not driving anywhere."

"I don't care. I want you. And I want you now."

"Sweetheart..."

"Don't argue with me," she said, digging her nails into my hand. I've felt it before, and I never was too happy with her scratching, whether playful or serious, and I knew her long enough to know that whenever she had too much, she did it to hurt. To see me bleed. To draw a sexual monster out of me vengeful enough that I would make her bleed back or make her submit to a finality so amazing that she would let it become her instead of just a temporary pleasure that she would borrow, then let go. She had wanted me to ravage her. And I did not. Solely for the reason that the night would become just that - a sex mission - instead of what it was meant to be - something personal rather than physical.

"Please don't do that," I said.

"What's your problem?"

"I just don't want you to do that right now."

"This?" She said, coyly, and did it again. This time I pulled away from her and put my aching hand back on the counter to grab my beer glass.

She was now full of hurt and frustration. "What the fuck is wrong with you? Don't you want to fuck me?"

"Babe..."

"No, don't even do that. Don't play that game. I'm not in the mood for names. I'm in the mood for you to hurt me. I'm in the mood to be taken over. Don't be such a pussy."

And I was at that point where my temper - my father's temper, which was never a peaceful thing - started to take over. If she wanted some of me, it would have to be this. And like I said, I am not proud of much, but this may be the one part I wish was buried. Under concrete.

"Quit acting like a baby. Just because I don't want to fuck you now doesn't mean I never do. And just because you have a few drinks doesn't make you queen of everything. You just need to relax."

"Who do you think you're talking to?"

"I'm talking to you. Knock it the fuck off. We had a perfectly fine evening and you're making into this pity party of shit. And I'm tired of it."

"If you don't think i'm pretty tonight, you should have just fucking said so."

*And she was. Believe me. She had everything. She was every kind of word that my own language could not describe. Her skin. Her hair. She was an entity that I was never blessed with before, and I wanted to swallow her whole, do things to her that no man could ever do to a woman. But I wanted to do it on my own time, my own want, my own desire. I couldn't let her have the upper hand on me. I couldn't let her hurt me and then let her run all over me. I've seen it happen. With my father and my mother, seeing how they were never happy and how they divorced as soon as it was brought up. Ruin was such a central force in my life and I didn't want to see it happen with her. Things were just too perfect at this time. But if I let this continue, she would fire every bullet in me until we were both exhausted. Finished. Panting, grasping for air, trying to reconnect on something futile instead of just taking our pride and letting common sense win out for once. But I couldn't see it going this way. It was bound to get ugly. It's just how it was. And I felt sorry for her.*

*"Fine," she said, breaking the silence. "You go home. I'm staying here. I'm not done drinking yet."*

*I didn't want to fight. I just took a few twenties out of my wallet and laid them down on the counter in front of her. I stopped to say something nasty, but decided against it, and walked out of the bar. Or so she thought. I waited until I knew she was looking away or texting someone, and I snuck back in and managed to go to a corner where I could see her very well, but she couldn't see me. I couldn't just let her there by herself. That I could never forgive myself for. And I guess this is another not-so-proud moment of my relationship with her in that briefly - despite our date night going so well beforehand - that I neglected to trust her. Our marriage. Our being together. It all became woven in doubt just like that, and I was going to make sure that even though we were at this part of the night, that she would be loyal. That she would realize that this was love at stake, not just some cheap fuck.*

*For a while, she did nothing. I saw her put her face in her hands and exhale loudly. I saw her wave trembling hands through her hair and debate on what to do. Several times I saw her pick up her phone, either to call or text, but put it back down again. She was at a boiling point herself, but it was hard to tell what she was going to do. I started to feel guilty. What the fuck had I done? How childish was I being? I had made such a stupid decision - she probably thinks I left her at the mercy of drunken strangers and I would be hearing about it for weeks at a time. There goes the dates, the dinners, the drinking, the hanging out, all to replaced by silence so* explosive that I would crawl out of my skin. I wanted to move but I went numb. I had wanted to die, the pain was so intense. My drunken body, my soaked mind - I had become awash with regret and stupidity, and just before I went to move out of the dark corner, walk up to her, grab her by the arm and lead her to the car, something unexpected happened.

A young college kid, probably on his first night out binge drinking, sat next to her at the bar. He was nondescript in every way, but he was existing next to her, and that was enough to make me want to kill him. But instead, my pathetic psyche took over and whispered just to trust her. See what she does. Temptation. How would it go? What would it do? And as I shook my head and took in a deep breath to steady the swirling room, I questioned my motives. What was I doing? Why wasn't I in bed with her to begin with? Why didn't I just leave?

At first, they didn't look at each other. The kid put his empty glass down on the counter, requested another. She stared at her phone like it was a wishing fountain. She didn't scan the bar for me. She may have welcomed the company. The kid got his drink, took a few sips, reached for a cigarette. He wrestled with the lighter and it was dead. He looked all around for his buddies, didn't find him, and sighed. Then, he turned to her, and must have *asked her for a light. We don't smoke, so she shook her head sharply and angrily. She was embarrassed. She must have sensed this as a pickup routine and didn't want to play into it. But yet she didn't move. My heart was racing. I began to feel sick. The bathroom was across the room, and I didn't want to risk being seen, at least not yet. A little wave rushed through me and I threw up into my hand, quickly wiped it on my pants. I was feeling like shit. And I wanted this to end. But I still couldn't move. I was fucking myself up by just standing there, breathing.*

*After a few minutes, he started to talk to her, politely. She must have been answering him because he began to nod, smile. It started to get a little more involved. She put her phone away. I pulled my phone out of my pocket to see if she had messaged me; she hadn't. And yet I still couldn't do anything. I was making myself into some sort of spy for nothing, and I debated on emerging, but then he must have made his move, because she shook her head, once, fast and started to get up. He must have put on his best routine, because he looked hurt and pissed off. He took a quick slug of his drink and started to get up, but one of his friends came up to him and patted him on the back. Seeing this as her getaway, she shoved the money I gave her back in her pockets, and ran into the bathroom., The kid threw up his arms in a frustrated gesture, but then* shrugged and paid for his drink, and then started to leave the bar.

That may have been the longest thirty seconds of my life. What was I going to do? Wait for her to come out, sit her down, apologize, and then let her fuck me? Was I going to be screamed at in front of everyone? Was I going to talk to her and tell her that I didn't trust her and that I watched the whole thing and that I was a paranoid piece of shit? Instead I did something both cowardly and heroic.

I went outside.

I spotted the kid getting into his car. He had been by himself, so he must have been not drinking too much. His friends seemed to have disappeared or popped around the corner to have a smoke. He started the car, paused to look at his phone, and that's when my blood had hit the fire it almost never does. I became rage. I became everything I hated. I really almost let this piece of shit win. I trembled. I couldn't think. My body, as drunk as anything, not even moving correctly to walk or think, became a weapon that I almost never used. I somehow made it up to the car. I swayed. I tapped on the glass.

The kid turned to look at me, saw me, puzzled.

I punched right through the glass into his face.

Blood became the color of the scene. My knuckles ripped open and my skin became lost from my body. His *face exploded into directions so quick that it amazed me - his nose twisted sideways and spilled its blood, his lips tore open in new patterns and spilled its blood, his eyes became shut and drowned with its blood, and his screams opened up the night. Glass stuck into my hand and stuck out like my own mistakes as his half became covered in glass as well, and he leaned back in his seat, moaning, bleeding profusely. I stood there, my hand dangling by my side, drunken and useless. I whirled around. No one heard me. No one saw me. I looked for her and couldn't find her. Suddenly, a hand gripped my injured wrist, and I turned and saw the kid trying to fight back. I hit him again with the other fist and he doubled over this time, blood and nausea becoming him. I stuck my head in the car as he moaned in pain.*

*"Get the fuck out of here, and never look at my girl again."*

*He looked at me as if I were death itself, and I don't remember him leaving, because I began to throw up in the parking lot - beer, water and anger flowing out of me like words, and it burned so bad that I sat down in front of my mess, picking bits of glass and blood off of me. I looked up at the sky and saw the stars, wondered how they felt from seeing this display of humanity, and before I* could get an answer from him, she had appeared in front of me, disheveled, worried, annoyed.

I looked at her and I held up my bloody arm. She swayed and stared at me, like she had never seen me before.

"I trusted you and this happened," I whispered.

She didn't get it, but I didn't expect her to.

"I should have just let you fuck me. I just should have," I started to say, and then the next thing I know, I'm in my car, and she's driving, and she's talking nonstop, frantically, about my blood, her blood, our blood all over the place. She takes me home, cleans me up in the bathroom. I tell her everything in a drunken spree, still sick and still on fire from the attack. I'm worried about legal activity. I can't even stand. And yet she still takes care of me, as I'm murmuring like a maniac, crying like a baby. I'm laying on the bed, holding my injured hand, wondering if it'll ever be the same, and she's riding on top of me, trying to get her fuck as if it's the last fuck on this planet. Night came, sleep hit me, and nothing else ever came out of it.

But the whole reason I share this story is because it shows the depth of how much I protect her. How much she is mine, when she isn't. She may never be again, but I still follow her on dangerous roads and unguarded paths, *attempting to love her like I did on this night. My reasoning is broken and she knows it, my logic is unfounded and shallow and she knows it, and just as stupid, stubborn and one-track minded she is, I know it, and that is what puts us in this situation. People say fate brings us to places where we adapt and live from it. I say it's the opposite. It's not the places that are fucked up. It's not home that's fucked up. It's people. Split second decisions are our downfall, and evil overwhelms us. Her traits and mine are a web, and it's not pretty. It's disgusting how we do it to each other. But just as much as I hate it, I love it. She's a story, she's a song, she's my everything, even a drunken beautiful girl who wants everything when I'm just happy with anything.*

I call her. I have to. The phone rings again and again. I know she knows this is my number. I have to see what happens. On the fourth ring, the phone is picked up. My heart briefly stops. There are games to be played from here on out and there is no official score.

First, there is silence. Then a fragile draw of breath. Then:

"What?"

"Are you alone?"

"Maybe, maybe not," she says in a vague, pissed off whisper.

"What is that supposed to mean?"

"What do you care if I am or not?"

"Because I want to know."

"I think you lost your right to know what happens in my life now."

"That's not true. I'm still your husband."

"Only legally. But I plan on changing that."

She invests in a language wrapped in barbed wire when she is upset or in a mood of rage. Most of the times in our relationship, it was never directed towards me. But now it is. I don't know how to shield it or to shy away from it. It distresses me. I wish I had water. I could leave the car and let flakes fall into my hand and eat it that way. I have an eternal thirst. She has a plan to make sure I starve.

"I can always change myself. You know the idea of people changing."

"That idea runs out after three years. Much like you did."

"Don't you see I'm trying to make this work again?"

"Why do you want it to work now if it didn't before?"

"It did work before."

"So you say, so you say."

"Look, I don't know about you, but I don't want to dwell on the past."

"I'm afraid we must. It determines what we do now and what we do in the future. People say you should forgive others for what happened in the past, but...I've known you for a long time. I've seen your decisions go through generations." She stops to take a long drink of something. "And most of the time, there were setbacks. Mostly bad ideas. But I couldn't stop that. But now I am stopping you. Because your decisions involve me. And I want no part of them."

I stared into the fog, hoping she was just ahead and all I would have to do was walk twenty paces and she would be there, on the phone. She was on the other side of it, but in a universe of rationality and sensibility. Something I could not belong to until I finally redeemed myself.

"What if I told you that I just wanted to be friends?"

"I don't want any part of that either."

Silence. Then, she spoke.

"I haven't seen one person since you left," she said softly. She takes another long drink. Judging by her tastes, she is drinking red wine. I never memorized what specific kind and neither did she. We always walked into the liquor store and she chose whatever she saw first. As long as it was red – she liked how it reminded her of blood. White wine just seemed too snobby, she said. Like it was meant for monsters. But red wine was like catering to the plain and ordinary, like they were just replenishing themselves with it. It is shit like this that made me fall in love with her. Most men will not admit it, but I've been defeated, so I will. It's the little things. They will flood you.

"Why?"

"I don't know why. Out of fear, maybe."

"Fear of what?"

"You should know why," she bitterly spat out. I heard her rustle around. The game suddenly got a lot louder.

"I'm sorry."

"Fine."

Again, a moment of silence.

"You don't think that's sincere," I said.

"No, not at all. If the only thing you worked on in three years was to make your apologies better, then go back and do it again for another three years. You might do better next time."

"You're vicious," I whisper. Everything in my body is heavy.

"I have every right to be."

"I don't know what I was expecting. I knew you weren't happy. But I just thought your reaction would have been a little different. That's human nature, though."

"Yes, I suppose it is."

"I guess it went exactly the way you wanted it to."

"More or less. I could have dealt without being hit with a rock."

"That was an accident. I mean it."

"Ok. That I believe."

For one brief second, we had a warm moment. Maybe our union isn't as shrouded as we thought. I felt giddy all of a sudden.

"So what are you doing now? As a job?"

"I'm not telling you."

Back to the start. "Don't you see I'm just trying to make this be civil again?" I'm repeating. Or close to. I just wish that I was dead. So I wouldn't have to do this.

"I don't think it ever will."

"Time heals all."

"No, it doesn't. Doesn't heal death."

"Don't be so…" She's reading my mind. And I yell at her for saying what I'm thinking. I guess I'm not so great when it comes to perfecting conversations.

"You know what? I'm glad I hurt you at the park."

"What do you mean?" I tried to act like it didn't. But she knows and I know that it destroyed me.

"Are you kidding me? Standing there, waiting for you to try to kiss me. That brought me a lot of happiness." She was feeling it. I could tell in her tone that she was beginning to get drunk. I closed my eyes at the thought of her stumbling around her house, not knowing what things were, remembering memories, crying, me not being there to hold her as she talked about things she couldn't tell anyone. I missed being that dump where she put her secrets. I missed being there to see her grow with every confession. I thought I was crying again, but it was just the feeling of my veins collapsing from this terrible cold.

"I wanted nothing else but that." I might as well admit the truth to her.

"I know you did. Which is why I'm glad I hurt you so much. I think now you understand the full extent of what I did. The full extent of what you did. But don't you dare say we're even. Because we're not. And I don't trust you and never will and if you think you are ever stepping foot inside this house again, you are dead wrong. Do you hear me?"

"There are things there that I want."

That seemed to stop her ranting. She took a long, deep breath. Carefully, she said, "What would those things be?"

I didn't answer.

I heard her breathing. I could even feel her breathing as if it were coming from my own body. It sounded so intense yet delicate, like a flower burning away and losing its petals to the change of nature. It was a thousand things at once. I imagined her sitting two seats away from the actual lamp so she would be on the edge of light. I imagined some novel sitting at the table by her feet, bent and frayed. I could only see the position of the room change every so often with every drink of wine. I imagined it as a scene in a novel where some sort of important revelation will be made or found or lost. There are a thousand tides that are made in the minds of people every day, and whether or not they join and coincide is up to us. But they die out just as quick as passion and her and I cannot stop that. I just hope that at least, tonight, they'll meet again, just briefly, to maybe heal each other's wounds. I feel like what I'm saying to you is prose. I was no scholar. But I'm confident enough to think that I understand what is going on here. I'm just not happy. Do me a favor, please, and never reword this. Just let it go as it is: a jumbled mess of uncertainty and disorder. Because then the meaning will be lost: the snow, parking in the fog. Life's little details cast aside with no one to see them prove to be very heartbreaking for those who are searching for it.

"Where are you?" She suddenly grew very sweet and scared.

"I'm about a half hour away. I'm parked on the side of the road because of the fog."

"The fog?"

"Yes, I couldn't drive anymore."

I felt like we were having that connection again. I couldn't think about that too much. It would drive me crazy if I did.

"I'll have the front door unlocked," she finally said.

"Okay."

"But I need you to understand something, and I mean it."

"What is it?"

"You're not staying here. I'm watching you go through it. You have no privacy."

"Fair enough."

"I don't care if it makes you sad. I'm not catering to your every whim. I don't know why I'm letting you do this. But if it will make you go away forever, then so be it.

That's what I have to do. This isn't anything other than what it is. Don't make it seem – "

I had to cut her off. "Okay. I understand. I'm going to start driving over there now and -"

She hangs up on me.

I let the phone drop to the floor of the car. I imagine it will soon be covered in dirt and dried leaves. I watch the snow dance from the heavens in the backdrop of the fog. I brought my arms together in an effort to get warm, but I knew that I would not be until I walked back into my house. I thought about three years, how faint and blurry of a time span it really was. Where friends come and go, where enemies are made, when you do things that you don't really mean or that you can't do what you intend to do because of time or whatever else. I thought about what she could have rearranged in the house. If my things were really there. I let my heart beat for a while just to hear the old familiar sound of life coursing through the confined space of the car. I welcomed my pulse as I would an old friend. I let my blood work its way back into my fingertips as I started the car. Like I was doing it for the very first time, I reversed the car back onto the road, and ignoring the danger, I drove back to her. I thought about the past. Continuously, I kept going back to when we moved in together. We were so healthy. We were so definite. But now, we're perpetually tired. Lost people lying on their backs with no pillows as we count the bumps and scrapes of the ceilings and floors around us.

I'm fortunate to feel pain so I can teach others.


She was sitting on the front step and she was covered in snow. She was wearing a torn red college sweatshirt and her hair was everywhere. I'm willing to bet any amount of money that she was very close to, if not already, drunk. Her hands were together and folded at the right knee. She was wearing thin black leggings and no socks or shoes. She was looking off in the distance to the left. I'm sure I blinded her with my headlights, but if it bothered her, she didn't show it. Maybe she loved the blindness. Maybe she loved pretending. She always seemed like an actress, deep down. She never went for it. She always went with what everyone else told her. I still think she still has a handful of dreams that she keeps in a jar, and when no one's looking, she brings them out and weeps, but does nothing about them. Maybe that was because of me. Maybe that's because I was a huge part of them and she can't be happy about them because I'm there and I'm looking back and forth at her, watching her as she watches me. Stare down.

She was still looking away when I stood right in front of her at the step. I wanted to cradle her in my arms and give her a new beginning. I wanted to rebuild the structure together and show her that a building can be fixed up at any given time. I wanted to tell her that in your youth we do really silly things, things that fall apart the minute we put them together, but I know that she would just tell me that she knew and that she didn't doubt it, and that we would be back at square one, like we were in a movie or something. We just didn't have a plot. We improvised.

Cut to dialogue.

"Hey," I finally said.

She slowly turned her head toward me and a good amount of snow fell off her hair and onto the ground at my feet. I watched as white sparkled in spots of her hair, on her face, where droplets of wet clung to her lips and her cheeks as her cold red patches of skin shone like flashlights in the silent, lonely dark. I watched as the universe let go of its bearings calmly on top of our house, as the rain gutters filled up with snow and cold, as the windows shook and froze from the wind, as both of our bodies were trying to find warmth all the way down to our broken nerves. She closed and opened her eyes several times over, as if trying to burn an apparition away from her sights. I knew she believed in ghosts. But she probably could not believe in this one. I think that through all of what happened; I made her reevaluate herself in terms of what she saw as real and what she knew as fake. It's a horrible thing to do someone after they spent all of their life trying to figure out things, because you and I know that it takes a very long time to hold something in your hand and confirm that it's alive. Like someone's hand. Someone's lips. A piece of their history that they trusted you to keep and watch over when you're gone. Like a diamond ring. Like the institution of living together and making vows. It's crazy. I watched as she went to open up her mouth and instead tasted the falling snow.

"Cold," she muttered.

"Are you okay?" Dumb question. But it progresses things like none other.

She nodded slowly as if the cold prevented her from moving her slender neck a certain length. I never knew her to stand so still before. She was always going somewhere, like someone was catching up to her during a long run, or someone chasing her to get something very important or valuable. But she always had value in moving. I never knew her to not go for a one mile walk every morning by the town's edge, along the river and through the thin patch of woods, down the railroad tracks…I know you don't see what I mean. But I'm picturing it like it just happened yesterday, even though I haven't seen it in so long. Maybe she's too scared to move. I wish she would move. I don't want to have to move her. I mean, I want to, but I know that if I pick her back up to go to bed, she won't want me to do it. She will get angry and claw at me and scratch me like she did once before when she got really drunk at a friend's house once. It was for a birthday party that wasn't hers, and at the time, she believed it was because she drank so much. I went to lift her up to take her to the closest bedroom, but she dug her nails into my neck so bad I had to get stitches that night. So I won't dare touch her now. I think it's because she has to put up with so much in childhood. She's so independent. She has yet to collapse. I don't know, maybe childhood has nothing to do with it. I can't sit here and form theories about things I don't know anymore. It's just a matter of making sure she doesn't ruin herself anymore over this blurry, unrecognizable past.

"I'm fine. Just a little cold."

"I know, it's snowing."

"I don't want you here."

"I know you don't. But you promised me that I could come back in here and get the rest of my things.

And you've been drinking, so I'm not staying that long because…"

"You won't know what I'll turn into?" We can still finish each other's sentences at a second's notice. It's either a skill we inherited or stole.

"Yes," I said, nodding. "I have no idea what about you has changed. But I'm not about to find out." But yet, I wanted to.

"Was it because of another woman?"

"No."

"Was it one of my old friends?"

"No."

"One of your old friends?"

"No."

"Someone you randomly met?"

"This is not another woman."

"Then who did you go for?"

"No one."

"God, you're a liar."

I cursed her name and she continued.

"There's another woman who's prettier than me out there. Who you decided was smarter than me. Who you decided was more beautiful inside and outside than I could ever be, and you wanted to be a part of her growth, and you said that one day, I will be with her, even if I have to destroy and mock everything that I had before."

"That's not true."

"And you ran into her and you decided that yes, I have to do this, even though it goes against anything else I've previously done in life. And what hurts me the absolute most is that you made this decision to be with someone who was so much better than me. I can't stand knowing that fact that you left me for someone who is greater than me in everything else. She can probably kiss better..."

"Stop it."

"And you loved every minute of it, but the guilt brought you so much pain, all the way down to the bone, and your real intention was to come back and rub it in my face. That's what happened. I decided to make the decision myself instead of wait for you to tell me, because if I left it up to you, I would be waiting my whole life." She paused to eat flakes of falling snow.

"No, that isn't true in the slightest bit. Get out of my way. I'm going in the house."

"No! It's not your house anymore."

"You're drunk."

"Stop saying I'm drunk!" She went to stand up, but instead stumbled and tripped into the snow. She clutched my wrist to keep from falling, but I wasn't a very good stopper. I watched her fall slowly into the snow and I laughed a tiny bit to keep the conversation going, but as she sat there, cross-legged, freezing, I couldn't help but think that if she did this to me, I might be doing the same thing – falling in the snow and acting drunker than I really was just so that I could still be able to smile.

"But you are. I can tell."

"You don't know what's best for me."

"At this point, I think I do."

"Leaving me was best for me, then, too, right?"

"Just let me in the house. Is the door open?"

"No, the door's not open. If it was, snow would fall in everywhere." Even when she was half gone, she still made these connections that would make sense to maybe children who asked a lot of questions, but to adults, it didn't matter to me much. Maybe she was a genius, deep down, and I just couldn't recognize it through the darkness of her mood. Either or, I just didn't want to put two and two together. I was done being a mathematician of relationships. I just wanted to be normal, and then leave.

"You and I both don't have all night to do this. So let's just get it done, ok?"

She looked up at me from the snow. Her hands were palm down in the snow, getting colder and colder as the flakes piled up on her fingers. I realized that now I'm constantly watching her all the time, as if she was my child rather than my wife. But maybe that's because at that moment, she looked very happy, not lost at all. She looked up into the sky as if answering a question from someone, but she closed her eyes and felt the cold bruise her. I just shook my head and started to walk into the house.

"Don't take your things."

I stopped at the doorway. I turned around to look back her in the darkness. "Why?"

"They remind me of you."

This stopped me for a few seconds, but ultimately, I just shook my head. It of course explains everything. "No. They have to come with me."

"But why?"

I struggled to think of an answer that she wouldn't drunkenly translate or misinterpret as being something else. It was hard sometimes to find a language that she would accept that reflected on her sobriety. I would always dance around those heavy questions, hoping that she would forget them in time if I just chose to let them die. I don't want to make it seem like she is a difficult person, because she really isn't. But at moments like this, when she says she's ready to move on, but then sits in the middle of the ground in the middle of the night and tells me something else, it's very hard for me not to break something out of impending frustration. It's in fact the reason I fell in love with her.

"Just get in the house," I said eventually. "You're going to catch a cold."

Surprisingly, she stood up and brushed herself off. She was soaking wet. A few cars drove past and she watched them before she started talking again.

"No, you're right. I don't want to get sick, don't I?"

She said it in such a soft murmur that I was taken aback by the sereneness of her voice. Maybe she was channeling the strength of the stars. Maybe she wasn't so much drunk, but just connected with the nature outside that she decided to show me what she learned. That was probably it, I assured myself. If I think of her in this unflattering light, then it'll make this next chore a lot easier. If I just think she'll stand there and watch the walls while I pack and not talk to me like she was earlier, than I would be out of here quicker than she would blink. What hurts is that this is the part of her that I love the absolute most – when she is so soft, innocent and carefree about everything. But yet, this is the part of her that I have to forget if she is to ever forgive me. I have to take the evil sides of her that would corner me in a moment's notice and choke me out, never give me a chance to regroup for a minute. I have to be just as tough as her if I want to get out of this. What is a nail, someone once said. A nail is but unison. Something like that. Maybe that's what it is. I'm making way too many generalizations. I just need to shut up. I'm sure you know what the exact quote is anyway.

"No, you don't. Come on. Take my hand, I'll pull you up."

"I can get up myself, thank you very much. I don't need you helping me all the time."

"Fine."

But she made no move to get up. Sick of waiting, I left her out in the snow.

Walking in, everything remained exactly the same. Not a speck of dust anywhere – she was and I guess still is a meticulous cleaner. The same paintings on the wall, ones that I never really understood but just accepted them as art and nothing but for her sake – all by friends of hers from college. And surprisingly enough, my contributions for decorations had stayed up – my grandfather's picture of the dogs playing cards, an old dream catcher I bought at a festival, a tattered poster of my brother's first gig in the living room – was all there, waiting for me again to give my greetings. I walked up to my brother's poster. I just stared at it, like it was a nightmare or some weird epiphany. I just couldn't believe it. My breathing started to get really sharp and quick and I couldn't figure why. I walked through the rest of the living room.

Nothing was changed. A glass coffee table. Old little trinkets I've picked up over the years stay dormant on wobbly wood shelves with weakening fasteners holding them up, as if the walls were bearing prideful yet tired children. There was barely any light on in the room – just the velvety drone and whine from the TV. A crumbled up newspaper on the floor. A bent book. Pencils next to paper next to other pieces of paper next to bracelets and shoes. I sat down on the couch and felt her warmth – this is where she was probably sitting when I called. A wineglass by the edge of my feet underneath the table. I was right. If I knew her, the bottle of wine would be underneath one of the pillows next to the arm rest of the couch. And there it was. Her favorite. I just let it back in the same spot – it was her comfort zone and I had no right to intrude. I looked out of the living room window and still saw her sitting in the snow.

She wasn't doing anything but watching the road. This late at night, only a handful of cars would lumber fast and disappear even faster into the night. Sometimes, when she couldn't sleep, she would stand by the bedroom window and just watch silently. She never explained why, but I guessed it was because she just needed something to keep her mind on and it was an escape. I realized now that it must be an even greater one since there was a huge, ugly void she needed to fill in my absence. She must have memorized colors, models, makes and even engine sizes. I guess she was just waiting for one certain car to come into her life, pop her misanthropic bubble, and remove her from the house, to go on roads yet untraveled or seen. I think about her flaws a lot, but never choose to focus on a specific one and completely unravel it. I wanted to open the window and throw her a coat, or remind her that her favorite show was coming on, just so she could snap out of her moment and come back to reality. I decided against it, though, simply because she would not listen to me.

I went into the kitchen and poked around, but nothing was changed. I didn't know really how to handle it. It was like I just got back from work and everything was waiting for me like it used to be. It's funny how demons stand still when you expect them to move so fast around you that both they and you get really dizzy. You expect them to possess you and haunt you, make you suffer and hear really strange voices, but in the end, they leave no angry or jealous footprints or lasting images or impressions. They're just there to watch you and that's it. I don't see how people can let them be ruined by these things. We have the power to block them out entirely on occasion. Her demons right now were definitely talking a hold on her. But, then again, I have to keep reminding myself that she is drunk, and that I have to get out before she finally snaps, like really gnarled, tired old wood.

I walked up the front staircase, thinking she would come follow me. But she did not. There were only two rooms up there – the bathroom and the main bedroom, where the majority of our lives took place. Most of my things were in a desk in that room – I didn't have a study like I pretended I did, but it was my little corner where I went to escape. But there was no sense in escaping in that room. Everything happened there. We ate up there, talked up there, argued up there, dreamt up there, held each other during scary dreams up there. It was a safety land for us – where nothing could really rip us away from our rooted positions. Yet, both of us now are detached and lost, looking for something to grab on to and wishing for some form of story that would make sense and help us sleep. I quietly pushed open the door for it creaked very loudly and for some reason, annoyed the hell out of me. In darkness, our bed lay like a monster, eating shadows, not moving, restlessly yet wearily breathing at the same time in some state of indifference. I flicked on the light switch.

Clothes everywhere. This is where, I should have guessed, most of the wrath and the breakdown had been spent. Nothing was left untouched. The bureau was chipped and pockmarked in many places. Most of her clothes and toiletries and jewelry were scattered about, like they were all playing some game of war with each other on the rug. Most of all these things held a bitter taste for me – they were parts of her that she fawned over, cared over, while most of my things, at least while I was there, were ignored. She was more into work than my own. I wouldn't call anything what we did work, but it was how we scratched out a living, so I guess the signifier of that word isn't as strong as I want it to be. There was my desk – also chipped and blanketed in her dirty laundry and other accessories. Other than my lamp, there was nothing else on it. Everything was in the drawers, unorganized yet in a system for only me to enter. I walked to the desk and remembered that the drawers had a lock. Like I never left, I instinctively opened up the small corner of rug against the wall and found the little gold key. It drove her nuts where I hid it. Either she figured it out in three years and let it go out of respect or was too busy driving herself nuts to try to pry open this chest and find hints and secrets. Maybe the truth scared the shit out of her. I know it did to me already. The truth is such a horrible entity – it is not peaceful or interesting, nor does it bring any closure to the realm – it's an albatross around the neck that feeds on bones until they snap or give way in your body and you have no choice but to lay down because the pain is so dead and great. It's not a wonderful feeling, as I didn't expect it to be, but it's something you just can't pass off as a fleeting instant. It sticks to you and clogs your mind. No surgery can undo it. Just as I was putting the key into the first lock of three, a noise startled me and I dropped the key onto the floor.

"So that's where it was this entire time," she said, confirming my curiosity.

I turned around and saw her. Dripping wet and shivering like the final leaf on a tree in an oncoming storm. Still, though, I can't say enough about her timidity and how explosive it was. It was enough to set the unreal city on fire. No maker could erase their work on her, if indeed, she was created by a higher being that we cannot see.

"Yes. I guess…you never decided to look."

"Didn't care enough to search. Can you hand me another sweater from the dresser?"

I did. I threw her one of my old ones that was three sizes too big on her, but she put it on without any fuss.

"And sweatpants, too."

I did as I was told. I didn't want to see her get sick.

"How much wine did you drink?" I said, returning to opening up the drawer. It popped open and there it all was. I didn't know what the fuck I was going to do with it.

"Enough."

"I guess that's the only answer I'll get to that. I thought you never drink by yourself anymore."

"Who else am I going to drink with?"

I sighed and grabbed all of the papers and stuffed them into a folder. "I'd rather you didn't to begin with."

"You're not my mother."

I turned around and she was drying herself off with a towel. I resisted every urge to just start over with her. Quit acting like we were in a play with the angry dialogue. Just throw this script away and have a new beginning. I wanted nothing else, believe me. I was tired of spinning on a crazy cycle. My eyes were starting to get really tiring. The bed looked comfortable, but it would be foreign to me. I wouldn't know how well I would sleep. I kept going through the drawer and found photographs of my family. What was left of it.

"No, I'm not."

"Did you fall out of love with me?"

"No."

"Did you hate the way I kissed you?"

"No."

"Did you hate the way I touched you?"

"No."

"I did my best to please you."

"I know."

"Don't be like this."

"You're asking questions that don't have answers."

"Yes, I am. Every question has an answer."

"Then why are you asking me these questions? What kind of answer do you expect to hear?"

"That's two questions."

"Fine. Why are you asking me these questions?"

"So I can figure you out."

"What kind of answer do you expect to hear?"

"Anything that will just make me understand you. I don't know who you are."

"No, it's still me."

"I know it's you, physically. The same face, the same hands. But inside. That's a map. That's something…that just seems so odd to me…"

"Believe me; it's not easy for me either."

"Am I confusing too?"

"No, you're not. You're one of the simplest people I know."

"Is that why you left?"

"What do you mean?"

She sat on the edge of the bed. "Because you're more complex than I am? Because you want more? You desire more? Do you hate the way I perceived your thoughts?"

"You have no idea what you're talking about."

"I'm just trying to figure you out on another level. Just trying to see past your mask."

"I have almost everything here. I'm leaving."

"Don't go."

"It's clear to me that I love you. And that no matter how many times I say it, whether you're drunk or sober, it'll never make things go back to the way they were. So what's the point? You're drunk, you made that decision."

"You know nothing of my decisions."

"Fine, then I won't say anything else."

"What the fuck are we doing to ourselves?"

"What do you mean?"

"We're acting like we're twelve. Talking in circles."

"I don't know. I'm not staying much longer."

"Do you know how many times I wrote down your name in the last three years?"

That comment made me turn around. She was lying down on her back wearing just her leggings and a t-shirt. The clothes I had given her were on the floor next to the wet towel. Her hair was splayed out all over her face and she was curling her toes. She was attempting to make snow angels on the crumbled sheets and failing miserably. Her body carried a faint vapor of alcohol; I could detect it in her muscles as she, in a fatigue, tried to stencil the image of an angel on our old bed. I shook my head and walked to the edge of the bed, staring down at her. Her hair covered her eyes; I couldn't tell whether they were looking at me or not. I was hoping she would be in a way. But another part of me hoped they were getting ready for bed.

"What did you say?"

"Hundred of times," she muttered. She stopped making snow angels and sat up. With a hair flip, I now saw her face. Still soft, still smooth, bearing years of practiced beauty and wonderful care. There was a secret to staying forever young that scientists would be searching for but she has found it. I don't know how she goes about doing it, or what kind of steps she takes, but she is more concerned about appearance than anything else. I knew that she always stopped to look at her reflection in a mirror, no matter where in the world it may be. She never missed what was going on behind her, but she knew she was beautiful. I wanted to take my finger and trace the bones around her eye and her cheek, just to see if I still had memorized the diagram. Over the years, I could have gone to it blind like Braille. Now it took me forever just to see the surface. I realized that the reason I'm commenting on her beauty like this is because she's letting me see this hidden side of herself – she is choosing what side of herself to bear to me right now in her moments of desperation and serenity. She is right now becoming the master of midnight separation – what part of her soul she's keeping away from me and what part of her soul she's letting me wrestle with.

"You wrote my name down? Why?"

"So I wouldn't forget it."

"You're crazy."

"No. It shows how much I was in love with you."

She sat up and leaned against the baseboard of the bed.

"My own name sounded weird to me at times, because it was a substance. Or rather, an element. But your name was so different. I had trouble pronouncing it at times. Even in my dreams, when someone asked me what your name was, or when in that one dream I filed that missing persons report, the cop behind the counter asked me what your name was. I had to write it down. But all that came out was just...nothing. So I woke up the next day and I filled up an entire notebook. Of nothing but your name. I managed to get my lips to say the word right. But then of course, you weren't around to hear what I had done. So...I told no one. And saved the notebook. And then I threw it out because no one would understand the true extent of my work. Say it with me. Say the name with me."

I was starting to not see who this person was. I didn't understand why she had done it. It was almost as if we traded personalities when I drove into the fog.

I dropped everything I was holding at the foot of the bed. These were things that I worked for – even though my family had shattered like glass and all of my hard work in college only resulted in a bookstore job – were still nuts and bolts that made up my machine of dreams and of the past. I couldn't doubt its existence for a minute. That's why I put them on the edge of the bed for her to see. I needed her to understand why I sweat so much, why I drank so much in school, why I cried about my parents – all of this was far more important than some notebook being filled with my name. If I was selfish, I'm not apologizing. This was realism as its best. At this point, I cannot and will not apologize for doing this. I refuse to.

"Look at this."

She did. "What's that?"

"Work. I've suffered for this. Something you never understood."

"And you didn't understand my work." She leaned in and started to get incredibly defensive. I could see that this was pointless. I might as well just take all of this to the grave with me because it obviously wasn't going to get through to her. It was just a foreign language to her. I scooped all of the papers, but before I could do anything else with them, she jumped up from the bed with incredible speed, snatched the papers out of my hand and tore them up into little pieces. When she was done, she threw them up into the air and it rained down camera paper and other things down on to us – lovers in a weird style of rain. I stood in shock. All of what I had kept here hidden for years was suddenly just destroyed in front of me, and she chose not even to look at one of the reasons why I had come back. Something important like that I had figured she would love to see. She crossed her skinny arms and just smiled at me, as if to say, my turn next. I wanted to strangle her. But for some reason, I felt at ease. I felt like she lifted a gigantic stone off of my chest. But at the same time, I couldn't thank her.

"Why did you do that?"

"So you can see where I'm coming from," she said.

"I saw what you were trying to say."

"No, you fucking didn't. You looked at me like I was crazy. I KNOW that look. I KNOW what you're trying to say when you give me those kind of glares. You must have thought that I had no idea what I was trying to say. Jesus, that's why you walked out on me! You thought I was insane! You thought that I was losing my mind! I was trying to be the perfect housewife all the while trying to make a career – "

"Stop! You are not insane. Neither of us are."

"How can neither of us be insane? We're human, aren't we?"

I stopped for a minute. She was right. No matter what we do, we are perceived as much because of strangers constantly being in our lives. Something that may seem right to us is weird to others. Other people orbit us like stars the second we leave our houses to go live our lives, and people see us get into cars and eat food and carry bags and they stop and wonder why we're doing it like this or why we're even doing it all. Humans, I suppose, are crazy. They cry and get pissed off when they can't be. When they're forced to abide by invisible standards set by others, they secretly rebel inside their heads and wait for the right moment to unleash it out on those people. I guess what she was really saying that even though we did what we thought would be helpful, just turned out to be the actions of our sanity fucking us over once more and letting us to rework the figures without a second chance. If this was the case, then all of our trying to make things better was futile. We should all just have lived in a padded room where we believe that happiness is just another buckle away on the straitjacket. Where bouncing souls meets lowered expectations and we never have to pretend again, where we can live out the fantasies like another day of the week.

"Yes, we are human. I guess you're right. I can't argue that."

She picked up the tattered remains of my family photos. "Why did you want to keep this?"

"I don't know. Because it was something about me that I cared about so much."

"It's nice to start over. Once in a while you just have to start over. Don't carry this shit around forever.

Like you. I carried you for so long, but I'm done now. I have obviously no feelings left for you. They are all gone. I had to kill them because I had to start over. If you expect to carry this shit with you the rest of your life, then you're fucking nuts. All of us are. If I was going to spend the rest of my life with you in my head, then I was going to jump in a river, and believe me, you are not worth suicide."

I smirked in spite of myself. The comment stung, but I have to live with it.

"You have to forget the past. It's not worth remembering."

"Unless of course you're remembering times with someone. Days and hours that you can't get out of your head."

"Well, there is that," she said, dropping the photo remains. "In time, though, that goes away. It will for you."

"Maybe getting your face out of my memory, but that's not going to change how I feel about you."

"Your opinion of me is lessening. You can't fool me. I'm drunk and I just ripped up your photos and your work and everything you cared about."

"Love blinds you."

"It kills you, too."

"Well, there is that," I said, repeating her, and again, smiles at the same time. My heart again leaped. It felt like we were running through the domestic motions again, like we were rehearsing for so long and this was a performance. But this wasn't in front of anyone but ourselves and that made it a lot harder and just a little more painful.

"It absolutely destroys you," she said, leafing through what was left of some of my college papers. "It makes you wish you belonged in someone else's skin, even if that person is far worse than you are. I hate being in love. Maybe I hated being in love with you. I hated it when people came up to me and gave me sympathy and pity and all of that other shit. It was useless. Why would they be sympathizing with me on love when they're exactly the same position I am? It's horrible. You're horrible and I'm horrible. It makes perfect sense to me now. I didn't need your explanations at all. I realized it all by myself."

"Then why are you letting me stand here? Why haven't you killed me or why didn't you just shut the phone off? Why did you destroy what I had saved for so long?"

"You're asking me questions," she slurred, "that have answers I don't give a shit about."

"You have to care. It's something that you have to care about. You can't start this over. It stays with you for so long. You can't get rid of something like this."

"I'll teach myself how to."

"Don't. It's pointless."

"And you know what's best?"

"No, but I know what to do. I had to move on. The reason I stayed gone for so long is because I needed to get over you. I love you now, because I realized what I left behind. But at the time, I left because I was only in love with the idea of you."

She glared at me and repositioned herself on the bed. Her nails were digging into her legs and I feared she would draw blood because she was pressing so hard onto her skin. Not even layers of the toughest material could stop her if she wanted to bleed. She would find a way. Determination overrules anything else when you're fighting to understand the person you love and why you love them.

"You were in love with the idea of me?"

"Yeah."

There was a pause. I thought for a second she would dematerialize or have all her bones broken in an instant because I told her what I had finally felt. Maybe she would go into shock because I confirmed that her purpose in this world was not as strong or meaningful as she had hoped it to be. I didn't want to tell her in those words, but it would be better if I did, simply because in any other way she would not understand. I was destined to keep ruining her life. One day, our bond would be erased legally, and everyone would act as if we were never married at all. But in moments like this, nothing can change the fact that we did stand in front of each other eternal bliss. It seems so strange now that we're doing this. But as a game of life, it's okay. Not every game will come out with all winners. Someone has to lose. I wish our creator would have written easier rules or rewired our hearts to accept crushing defeat and loss of trust.

"I want to say I know what you mean, but I don't."

I sat down at the edge of the bed. She shrank back to the baseboard and sat Indian style. I pushed all of the torn scraps off the bed and onto the floor – I would clean them up before I left.

"I won't come any closer," I said.

"Good."

"I'm going to try to word this in the best way possible..." I paused, maybe out of some outside chance that something else would interrupt me. When nothing like that came, I decided to look at her and tell her this instead of watch anything else. I would probably want the same done to me.

"When I first saw you, I didn't know what to do. I remember that day. I was scared to death in coming up to you and telling you anything. I remembered how you smelled, what you wore. I remember saying to myself that when I talked to you, I wasn't going to let you go. For anything or for anybody. I had heard of you through so many of my friends and I just wanted a moment to get so close to you. You had an aura. I'm not going to lie. I was completely fascinated by how you structured yourself."

"Was I pretty that night?"

"What?"

"How pretty was I?"

"Absolutely magnificent. You had darker hair then."

"I did? I don't remember."

"It's ok. I do. Anyway, when I saw you...I knew that I wanted to be with you. But as time wore on, I realized that you were far better than anything I could ever be. Or deserve, for that matter. But I went after you anyway because love makes you blind. Disgustingly blind. I realized that by the way that you were, and how you thought so much better than me, that one day, you were going to be far beyond anything I could ever comprehend."

"This doesn't give you reason to leave me," she whispered. She started to cry.

"I'm not done my story yet."

"Fine."

"Please, give me one more chance to talk, if this is going to be the last time."

"I don't see where this is going. This seems to me like you're just going to build this all up for nothing."

"You have to let me finish. This is what you waited to hear."

I expected her to say something back in sarcastic return, but nothing ever came. I took her silence and teardrops as a plea to continue.

"I married you because I felt that I could be on your level some day. I had hoped you loved me the same way I loved you. I loved you unconditionally. Whoever says that is impossible is dead wrong. I never judged you. I just knew that you were so much greater than me in everything we did. All of your friends said it. Even all of my friends said it. There was no way I could deny it."

She said my name in a plea.

"You know what I mean, though. Everyone knew you were way better than me. And the pressure got to me."

"I was never better than you or anyone else."

"See, my explanation is getting screwed up because this isn't the way I wanted to tell you. I can't describe it. There's no way I can put this feeling into words. All I know is that when you kissed me is when I felt it the most. That in your lips was when you were trying to pass some of that along to me and I just never caught it because I was more wrapped up in the physical beauty of it. Do you know what I mean? It was like what happened in the park earlier. When you went up to me and tried to kiss me. At that point, I was so close to understanding you and being like you, but then you pulled away and killed it for me. Does this make any sense at all?"

I wanted to believe that deep in what remained pure and whole of my heart that this was a beautiful moment in our lives. Forget the fact that we had just ended a holy marriage; forget the fact that we are on the verge of taking one weapon to each other's face to make nothing there at all, forget that the fact that for years we disappeared inside of ourselves and didn't tell the other a fucking thing, I just wanted this to be precious. I wanted us to hold hands as I dug deeper and deeper to make sense of the time I was spending with her. She was obviously in need of company and I just wanted one more chance to make clear my intentions, for they really were for the best in the end. I wanted to pour her my beauty and give it to her so she could have seen some of mine for a change. I wanted to hold her drying hair in my hand and whisper to it so it would wake back up again and roll with the wind as we walked outside and noticed all of nature in this horrible city.

I was thinking again in prose because she does this to me. When she looks at me, the floodlights to my mind just open up and spill out everything I've thought about in the past few hours. Or years, at this point. Years of holding back pressure in my body to tell this fucked up world how I felt and where I stood among the masses of people who said they were in love, but never made the effort to tell anyone about how they felt. Where I lived the last three years, no one understood this. I didn't expect them to. But I'm avoiding the point I wanted to make. As she was looking at me with those incredible eyes, I just wanted to reach into them and show that yes, this was a beautiful moment, for once, that contained nothing but authenticity and honesty, and this may be the last time in our insane, pathetic lives that we feel something real again. Because of that, I wanted to believe this was beautiful – something you would put in a book somewhere. Something that you and every one in my life would appreciate. I went to grab her hand.

She accepted it, but carefully. It was a start.

"You couldn't fall in love with me because I wasn't…like you?"

"No, that's not what I mean. Because I wasn't like you. You were fine. It was me."

"Every man says that when they break up with someone. 'It wasn't you, it was me.' When clearly it is the other person. Everyone uses that line."

"Well, I'm being sincere. I mean it. I need you to understand how this affected me and how it still affects me now. This isn't fully over. Shit, I don't even know if it's barely begun. This is something that will last for a long time and sadly, you and I have to live every day like this from here on because we're finally saying this shit to each other."

"It just seems backward to me," she whispered again, this time more sleepily. "How someone could love someone and then marry them and commit to them and then just walk out because they were better than somebody? Didn't you want to stay and get better? I would have helped you out. I would have been there for you and helped you do anything that you wanted just to make this work. I didn't want anyone to run away if they didn't have to. You could have stayed. Were you afraid of my reaction?"

"Maybe a little," I admitted. "I just didn't want you to run away from me because suddenly I felt inadequate and unworthy of anything you were giving me."

"How did you want me to react?"

I honestly didn't know. If only I could go back and start this over, replay the tape and record over the parts that I hated and replaced them with moments I loved. It seemed unfair, how things stayed permanent in a moment's notice. I thought of how you might tell others this. I thought of many things during this flash of time. But I was determined not to let anymore slip past until I convinced both myself and her that I was saying and doing was the correct action.

"I wanted you, I guess, to do something that I didn't think was possible. Which is accepting it. I don't know. I ran because I was scared. I didn't go for anyone else and I never did anything else with anyone. Why would I do anything else?"

"Because you were alone and you were convinced that you were out of love with me. You could have done anything you wanted without any eyes to watch over you. You could have ruined the world and set the universe on fire and not one goddamn soul would have cared or said anything because you believed you were out of love and when a man thinks he's out of love, then he can't do shit, and for that, I think you're the most spineless man who ever lived. You have to believe you're in love every second of your life and if you don't, then you have nothing to live for."

I let go of her hand and stared at her. She had floored me. Even when I thought she was down for the count and broken, here she was. Everything was black except for flakes of white. Explosions of ice and frost were sure to go off at any minute and I was certain I would be scraping my car in the morning or even a half hour from now. I thought about how almost everyone around us would be sleeping in the same bed and holding each other except for her and I. We would still be dealing with this. We would still have to clean up the living room, possibly tape back the photos and hope the tape sticks and never curls or falls off, wash out the glasses, put the wine back, and see it to that her doesn't get sick. If anyone calls me insane for living out my night like this, I will have to fight back. Maybe misaligned beauty and unsure feelings of love are just what helps me sleep at night. I don't think she minds by now. I felt a brief surge of weird happiness – if anyone had fucked me up, it was her, and vice versa. At least we fell victim to our own insane hands instead of anyone else's, for I think we would be in constant tears instead of this back and forth whispering that seems to feel more like a dream than a real moment. I wanted to kiss her, solely because she had stunned me. I was lost beyond belief in her safety. I wanted to think this room was a cage and the key was a thousand paces away.

She stared back. She knew she had me in her palm. What was I going to do? Was I going to fall or was I going to get up and let her get over this? I don't know. To this day, I still don't know. All I know is that you don't plan anything like this happening, ever. You just go along with the flow and hope that the wind is in your favor so you can ride it for a long time. You just hope and pray that when you get to a sidewalk and there's a stop sign there that it doesn't mean for you to stop, but rather, everything around you so you can keep going. I shouldn't be mad at her. I need to be forgiving and accepting of her even if she wasn't going to ever forgive or accept me. I needed to be able to sleep for the rest of my life knowing that. She had just had a perfect moment, and it makes me have hope for the future that we, as a civilization, have evolved to the point of understanding what beauty is, and to be able to tell someone else that they are right is a breathtaking step forward for humanity. I just wish I was on the same level of thinking as her, but I was failing miserably. She was the teacher now, I was just the student. Education really has no boundaries, and it's astounding.

She interrupted my train of thought. "What do you have to live for now?"

"I don't know."

"See what I mean? When you get that point, what is it worth?"

"I guess…to be forgiven."

"I couldn't forgive you right away."

"I realize that."

"Good. I need you to understand that. This is pain. You have given me pain. Instead of trust or anything else. You just left me pain. And problems that won't go away. Can I trust another man ever again? Time will tell. It'll tell me when the time is right, but you can't or I can't. See, you left my life in the hands of blind faith. Something that isn't reliable. You left me to depend on something that I can't hold. That's a nice feeling. I'm grateful. So see what you did? Invisible amounts of never-ending pain. You fucking asshole."

She put her face into a pillow and cried worse than anyone else I ever heard in my life. I've dealt with suicidal friends, people going through withdraw, my own family going through their stages of grief and dying with others, little kids losing their mothers – anything synonymous with loss I have heard and seen enough times that I should be able to write the proper script on how to cry. But nothing compares to this. It sounded something like sheet metal being punched over and over again, like hail crashing haphazardly against a tin roof, screeching and shouting against the weight of the world pressing down on its support beams and thinly shielded shingles. It was loud and it even hurt me. The three year sobs that had been held down because of stability and appearance now finally leaked out from her body in the forms of spastic weeping. Three years of turning over in your sleep, dreamlike, to reach for a familiar body and to come up empty handed – three long years of kissing the silence goodnight and putting your hands to your chin and imagining your lover's hand on the small of your back. Wondering where the fuck he was and why he was gone. Why suddenly you felt like a child and he went to the land of grownups. Now, finally, we were not strong. We were revealing our true selves. I was now to be the strong one, even for a few more minutes in my life with her. She would not want me back. I would love her unconditionally until the end of the universe, but she would forget me and eventually yearn for so much better, a person who didn't resemble the devil.

"I'm going to ask you one more time. And you better not lie to me because I will kill you right here where you stand. Did you leave me for another woman?"

I looked into her empty eyes. Her twin voids, staring back, flexing and pulsating its own special fire and anger. I answered the only way I could.

"No."

My heart stopped. It tried to beat. It tried to pump blood back into my body. It tried to make me feel better, but I was getting woe. All forms of happiness were starting to become eliminated from me. I was starting to become a new body. My heart was in the process of shedding its skin and to get a new membrane, a new cover, new nerves, new everything. I was to learn how to walk differently, talk differently, gain a new set of eyes and hands and feet, and remember only the memories and to start getting new ones, all because of what I had done. She only wanted to know this. She didn't care about a job or any new friends or any movies I watched and liked over ones I've seen with her. It was all about finishing the job – driving the stake through the heart, adding the final bullet in the chamber, getting that one last shovelful of dirt in before it started to rain so the mud would overflow and cover the world afterwards. She just wanted to know if I fell in love with anyone else, and if so, were they the reason that I had left. And I swear to you and all that I consider to be real – that is not the case. I left because I could not give her the attention that she truly deserved. She needed to be worshipped by someone else – and that was not me. It would never be me, even though I made that vow to. This was truly the end. I would live suspended, and she would just crash, and that was just the way it had to be until we were dead and gone.

"Ok."

I got off the bed and stood up to look out the window. In the time of this, the snow had calmed and ceased to exist. Maybe it knew that I was leaving soon. I hoped the fog would be clearing up soon. I just wanted to go back to home. I thought for a while that maybe this was home – maybe I would just be rejuvenated enough by coming back in here to stay despite it all. But I couldn't. There were things that I needed there that I couldn't live without, much like here. Maybe I give useless shit too much worth and value. That's just where I felt I belonged. It's so complicated. It's so pointless to try to make metaphors about the end of love. Who can truly say how it feels? It's different for everyone. Or home, for that matter. I can't spend the rest of my life writing about this or talking about this. It's simply what it is, and the only thing I can do with it is to give it you, one hundred percent, as if it was a being that needed care.

Don't expect any deep meaning out of this. Don't give it theory or second readings – in fact, when you get to the end, just throw it out and act like you don't know me. My name will be likened to that of other men that have left their wives when they needed them the most, and even though I won't like it at all, I don't have the power or the capability to change that. So there's nothing that I can do. But just act like I'm a part of the mist. Just act like I never existed and that this story came from someone else. It makes me feel like the worst person in the world – she is sitting on the bed, in pain, in tears, drunk, needing me the most and I'm staring outside the window and worrying about if there's still fog outside. It's not that my priorities are backwards, it's just that I seem to have none at all.

"I'm going to get going now," I whispered. She didn't respond and I turned around. She was in the fetal position, facing away from me. I walked around the bed, kneeled down, and moved the hair out of her face. It felt as soft and smooth as ever. I saw a face that resembled a Halloween mask. It was lifeless, numb – nothing could ever bring excitement back. She had been defeated at her own game. I saw the voids gaze at mine – once, a long time ago; this brought a smile to her face. Now, it was as if I just told her that infinity lasted forever. Nothing could surprise her or overwhelm her. I've officially ruined her.

I said her name. As quietly as I could. So she would have to hear me. So she would have to remember and use her shredded memory just one more time. I wasn't trying to feel violent or destructive. I didn't want to leave her broken and ruined. She was my lover, at one point. We had done so many things. I had touched her like she had touched me - we came into each other lives separately and finished off by connecting souls. And here I was - the one designed to end it. It was beautiful and it was ugly. But it was too late now. Turning back would be death, and she would kill me. It was just way too messy. I wished life wasn't so full of air. I'd be much better off choking and struggling somewhere. Maybe now was that time to find out what I could do without the air of life and love.

"What?"

"I'm leaving."

"Fine."

"I didn't lie to you."

"I know you didn't."

"Everything will be ok.

"No, it won't."

"Yes, it will."

"I wasted so much time for you. I can't care anymore."

"I'm going to still love you."

"I don't care."

"I do, though."

"Whatever."

"Maybe one day I will realize – "

"I hope you don't. I seriously, honestly, hope you don't."

I continued kneeling. I got an urge to roll her over so she could look at the snow on the ground, maybe look at more cars that drove past. But I left her go. This was her choice. As it was mine to leave. There was no sense in looking for anything else – it would be torn up, or I would look at it and just get sickened to my stomach and forget it. Nothing held any sentiment anymore. But it was really ok. She was right. Time to start over. I might as well, for one last time, look at her with my own eyes instead of a drunken dream or an old photograph. I moved the hair out of her face as she barely blinked at me. The alcohol was starting to get to her, she wouldn't be awake for much longer. I watched as her eyes fluttered.

She whispered my name, roughly, with great effort. She looked sick. And it was just enough for me to turn away.

"What?"

"Did you love kissing me?"

"Yes, I did. I loved it way too much."

"Do you remember the first time I kissed you?"

"Yes. Two months after that party. On the quad. I remember everything."

"It was the closest I got to feeling life," she whispered.

"What do you mean?"

"It was real. So real that I thought that it would always be there for me. But since it left, I forget what it was like."

"I'm sorry."

"Why would you do it one more time?"

"Would you want that?"

"I don't know. But my brain is saying yes. My heart is saying yes. I might as well say yes. One last glimpse at what could have been with you."

I don't think I could have ever argued with that logic. Looking back, I shouldn't have, solely because it really destroyed her. But I did because I was blind. I just wanted to give her that newfound life she always strived to achieve. I stupidly believed that I had it because I went missing for so long. But regardless of what was racing through my heart, I leaned in and I went to kiss her. I thought about what she did to me. There was no way I could do it to her. It was inhumane.

Our lips touched. Hers were still as full as the day I left. I never knew how mine felt as she never told me. But I felt the faint call of electricity when we started to touch. For a few seconds, they did not move – they hugged each other loosely as I breathed in the scent of her skin. It comforted me. All of a sudden, I tilted my head and she did the same as our lips locked tighter and I felt more of her lips with mine. She brought a hand to my cheek but I brought up my hand and put hers in mine. She had wanted it there, but I felt that it would be a better fit in my own hand. She tried to bring her tongue into my mouth, but I wouldn't allow it. I just wanted to kiss her. I didn't want anything special or amazing or life-altering – I just wanted to grant her the chance of one more kiss. Her eyes grew tighter – I opened mine just in time to see hers focus in the dark as she didn't want to see me, but rather, just imagine me doing it, so that it felt more like a dream that she would not wake up from if it ever came to her again. Softly, she brought her other hand to my cheek and this time I allowed it. It slid up my face and through my hair and for a second, I thought she was inviting me to the bed, but I didn't want to come.

I lost count of how many seconds we were kissing, but I definitely felt something there – I felt like I was that day where I waited outside of her macroeconomics class and she came out of the room in a wilted state – she had been partying the night before. She saw me and she wondered what I was doing there waiting for her, but I told her simply that I had a feeling that I should be here and that I should walk her to her next class. She accepted. I walked over with her to the science building and there was a fire in one of the labs – smoke flew out of the broken glass like birds. I took her by the hand and said that maybe we should just skip class for the rest of the day. Hours later, we had started a relationship. Moments like that reminded me why I was a human being.

We were still on the first kiss. I went to pull away so it would be over, but she wanted a second one. I opened my eyes again and her face was bright red, like she too, suddenly hated the air she breathed. She began to suck on my lips to the point where it started to hurt. I went to push away. She took her hand away from my hair and grabbed onto my shirt collar, trying to pull me in, to swallow me whole, to reabsorb love as a part of her functioning self. I pulled away with as much force as possible. As if she had been shot, she startled awake from the trance. I kept kneeling a few feet away while she had stared at me. I thought of that night where I refused to fuck her at the bar. It comes back to dominance. She wanted to be on top, even in this terrible state. It always comes back to this, doesn't it - the need to slaughter the more peaceful part of the puzzle for pure benefit. It's enough to liken relationships to war and no one ever wins. The heart, the head, it's all designed to snap.

"Get out," she finally said.

I started to say her name but she cut me off.

"Just get out," she said with tears in her eyes.

I stood up. I would have no need for any of this. I felt like I should have continued what I was going to say to her, but it would have been useless.

"Get out and please...don't ever call me, don't ever come back, don't tell any of your friends about me...and don't ever kiss me again, ever. Please get the fuck out."

I nodded at her and we met eyes one more time. She meant it. Whatever transformation or occurrence she just had, it was for real. This was it.

I walked to the doorway and looked back. She was lying on her back, her hands over her eyes, on the verge of passing out from the alcohol and the rush of love. I would never know what she did for three years, except for writing my name in the notebook. I would know nothing about her job or her family or her health. The only thing that I knew for sure was how bad she wanted to kiss me. How bad she wanted to feel and know what life was. I was the only person who could give it to her. In the weirdest case of loyalty I've ever known, I gave it to her because I am a giving person. It's just something engrained into me. I watched as she pulled the blankets up to her chin and briefly muttered about the light still being on in the room. I figured it was the least I could do. I let her watch outside the window for a few seconds before I shut the light off and closed the door, immersing herself in nothing but a wholesome quiet womb of black.

I went down the steps and shut off the TV. I drew the blinds. I put the wine away. I leafed through the mail on the kitchen table. I repositioned the couch, the pillows. I straightened out our vacation picture on the wall, her parents, and finally, our wedding picture. I made sure all of the doors were locked; all the downstairs lights were off, just like I did when I lived here.

With nothing else left, I left.

part

two

When I see myself, I see anger. I look in glass and find pieces of me that need fixing: I see desperation along with a clenched jaw, I see eyes that need a lift back into their sockets, I see a brain, that although functioning, ceases to work unless it has a lot of alcohol or pain to kick start it back into its proper ritual. Whatever the case may be, I see this face, and I want to die. I want nothing more than the skin around my nose and my ears to burn and drop off. I want piles of this dead skin to collect at my feet and be shells in the hot sand on the loneliest beach in the world. I want my footprints to disappear back into dirt so that no trace of me could be found. I want to become clear so that invisibility finally becomes a thing of the present. I want nothing more than to erase what I had learned over the years: love, commitment, friendship. I want to drown them in water that was not fit for humans to drink. I know these things are not real, and it would take a lot of daydreaming and black magic for them to come to life. But if they ever do, I hope they find me, and hone in on me like a missile: I want nothing more than destruction to these things, and I want it to come now, so I don't ever have to deal with the consequences of setting myself or my possessions on fire.

I want to become nothing more than this mistake that was put on Earth. Because when I walked through the glass of that mirror, I found something in myself that wasn't there previously: embarrassment. I had been rejected from people that I thought had loved me only minutes before. And then I see myself do what I did to her: I embarrassed her. But that was only after she had embarrassed me: we had evolved into nothing. We literally became lovers that did not care about anything except those unattainable goals we set for ourselves: money and attention and perfect love that could never happen. I see nothing but a cycle of embarrassment. I see nothing else I wanted other than death and poverty, heart attacks and lonely nights spent at bars: I was embarrassed to be a human, I was embarrassed to be this piece of shit that could never make anyone happy, and I had only done it to her because she had done it to me.

This is the part of the story I didn't tell yet only because I wanted to seem like some sort of martyr or hero. And now I know that when in storytelling, you can't lie: because the people you introduce later on contradict the hell out of you, and nothing is perfect, even in secrecy or concealment. And in those white-hot moments where secrets are born from places inside of you, in places where you thought they were so well-hid they would never run out into the open, they eat you alive, and those people exploit them, and you're nothing but a fragment of yourself, being watched by the people you love and judged by the people you hate. That's what happens to me now. I'm now watched by everyone. And it hurts and I don't know how to handle it, but if everything else comes out with the pain, then I might as well say that she treated me like shit, and if you want to not believe that, so be it, but in the essence of storytelling, at least now in my narrative, I can tell you this and get away with it: she had ignored me. I was beginning to die within, and she only chose to ignore it and focus on herself.

She was never always like that. She had loved me in the beginning. She worshipped the idea of a marriage and I went with it because I was in love. That's always how it begins – with pure blindness, flowers, and friends that surround you in support because they're too weak-spined to tell you the truth about the girl. You go through the motions and begin to sense flat lines the very minute you tied the knot, but you ignore it because you're drunk, or you're having sex, and you want so desperately to believe that there is power in her eyes, or love in her skin, and you move along with the curves of her body, and you go so deep within her that it's all so real, that nothing could ever be a dream anymore, that reality has crushed fantasy so easily that the most inexpressible is the most realistic, but you wake up the next morning and think that you just committed yourself to the one person who could kill you the fastest and the most silently. But she was not like that – at first. She looked at me with those open brown eyes and held my hand at dinner and stressed to me that college was not the greatest thing in the world, but love – and the skin of a lover, and the hands of a man who would hold her and lift her up even if she was drowning on land, and I had proved to her, apparently, in the time that I had known her, that I was the person that could save her shaky soul and give her some sense to live, even if her family and her career did not.

I broke her down from a human to a ghost. I couldn't see her as a human that did things that they would do. I saw her now as a specter that would float from friend to friend in daylight or at night, going back and forth between this person and this person in an effort to retain that kiss, or that moment, or the feeling of love or whatever it was she needed. I don't think she had bones anymore, or skin – in order to get over her, I had to picture her as famished, introverted, undernourished and bony, silent and small. I could not expect her to be in my dreams as much if she was just a mere thought instead of a being. When I left her in the dark bedroom, getting ready to sleep her intoxicated sleep, I had to leave her like that – I could not leave her normal, for I would have never gotten her confessions or secrets. So I can now finish off my thoughts of her the way I saw it. If she was lying down with the lights off, then I could not see her physically the final time I was actually around her.

Do I still love her? Yes. But will I live the rest of my life loving her and doing things for her? No. I have to keep her out of conversation. I can't tell a soul about anything she's done. If she's my problem, she's mine and mine only. No one else will ever have to hear about her again. I know that I love her and still in my heart, occasionally, there will be a sudden pang of regret or remorse or sadness sometimes, but afterwards, I have to get rid of it with something else. And usually that something else is a new chapter, or a new outlook, or maybe just to throw away things that remind me of her. It's like changing identity.

And sadly, that happened to me many times. More times than I would like to admit or remember. We change skins like animals. And we're proud of it.

Her and I could not cuddle or do the things that other lovers did perfectly. We weren't meant to go to dinner with others or sit and listen to our friends talk about their children. Lovers do things and they do them well. They try to do them insanely well. But I think we tried so hard that we missed the point entirely. We lacked the understanding of making things worth without any sort of hitch. We were too busy worrying about things way beyond our control to even kiss or wish each other a proper goodnight. Work was a nightmare. Worrying about the future, the environment – we never actually worried about each other, or asked each other how we were doing. We weren't definite lovers – we had pretended to be. One day, she read about them in a book during college, and she brought me along for the adventure and for a chance maybe, to study up on this thing called love, and see if we could do it like other strangers and friends. Yet, we missed the technical parts – the mechanics were rusty, the foundation was insanely weak. Simply put, she was intense and I was not. She had wanted things I could not give and I just couldn't give her things from the start. It's an eulogy. Think of it like that. It's a funeral procession of sorts. I talked earlier about caskets. We're not the ones who died. It's just what symbolizes us and makes us real. We can continue to be people who fight day by day. We're just not doing it together. Love is something worth waiting for, and even though fate hands us some really shitty cards, we just smile and say, "Ok, I'll wait for the next one." And eventually, as the odds will eventually be in our favor, we get that hand, and we smile, because it's the one we waited for. But not this time.

We had failed. Flat out miserably failed. Does this make me sad? It does. At this point in my life, and with my health and my job and everything else that I supposedly have left, I might as well admit some things about my sadness, because it's relevant to this story. More relevant than I wanted it to be, honestly, because this isn't all about me – it's the people in my life that I've been in contact with. This includes her and other people. Whether or not that I've touched them for the better remains to be seen, but I'm one of those people who wants to stay optimistic despite troubling times. But right now, I am sad. I'm sadder that I've ever been, because that kiss was the turning point of how I felt about everything. It summed up my definitions of love. It summed up all of the miles I spent driving around from town to town, looking for a stable place to live. Even now, at night, when it's absolutely beautiful out and covered in white, I'm still overcome by the feelings of failure. It's an attitude that I noticed before, but never really adopted. Now, though, it is mine. I am failure and sadness, in many different shades of colors and forms, and I'm willing to accept this. I have to see her like this, too, now.

Do you even want me to keep going on and on about her?

I don't think I should anymore. But this is a huge chapter in my life, one that I will always have dog-eared and marked, so I can go back with ease, or whenever I'm drunk, I can stumble to it, or whenever I have a moment where I'm about to lose myself entirely, I can go back and see her for what she is – soulless, just like me. She may be beautiful, but she is hollow – I have passed on my genes to her. She now has my problem of self-destruction and self-pity. Anything to do with negativity, really, She is now a master of. I'm a backwards teacher who does not carry the gift of progress. I'm stopping her from being truly happy again. She could have moved on entirely, started life over, moved with someone, married an actual man, not abandon any of her dreams, and done everything she ever wanted to do with her life. But she didn't. She cried and got frailer and frailer until there was almost nothing left of her. I'm sure she loved waking up every morning and looking out those same windows to see the same fucking buildings that were there years ago. Years of standing still and emotional deaths.

I can't spend the rest of my life talking about this woman.

I refuse to. There's such a thing called the future, and she's not included in it. But because we're human and we're inclined to fail at forgetting what we love, I need to decide on one memory I need to keep with me – store it in a locket, put it in a chest, commit it to memorization so I can fall back on it and so it can keep me from dying. Ok, here's why I want you to remember her:

A year before I left, we went to the beach – our only vacation. That was when we were at our healthiest in terms of everything. We got there as the sun was rising and we stayed there until the sun set on us as we lay sprawling in the sand with water waving in and out of our hands and feet. All day long, we had held hands and acted like these precious lovers we heard about. Not once did we fight, or bring up my parents or hers, or my brother or her sister, or anything else that could bother us. We walked on the boardwalk, got caught in a brief storm of rain, forgot our books to read, only had enough money for either lunch or dinner, and practically acted like we were young and restless. We were broadcasting amazing frequencies for miles upon miles, so people could see and notice how much in love we were. Time would eventually change this, but at the time, as we played and listened to music that only we could love, I knew that even though it was perfect, it could not last forever. I drove home with her sleeping in the backseat because she wanted to lie down. She saw all the sights before. This, I thought, was so noble of her – to leave everything to me as I led her back home, on these long dark highways and boring stretches of road that only had steel and debris. She had trusted me, and I loved every minute of it. That's why I want you to remember her.

But now we have to move on. As I drive, this woman is leaving my mind second by second. This is the slow, eventual death of my love. I have to spend the next half of this story on the other reasons why I left her, why I moved on, why I kissed her and left her.

This part hurts.

I got back to my apartment at three in the morning. All complete darkness, everything. For some reason, none of the lights work. I was shrouded in my silence that I paid too much money for. I made it to my room, stumbling in the shadows and grasping at the thin walls. I opened up my door and walked in to the only place where I really felt like I was myself.

There was no light coming from anywhere. I desired it as much as it desired me at the moment; one soul clutching for safety in the middle of a noise-filled night. I didn't mind at this point. My head was a cloud and I was certain that I was going to start sobbing like a little child any minute now. Pain registered as shockwaves; let my body know that I had one distressing day. I sat at the edge of the bed and undressed myself. In six hours, I would have to work and pretend to keep going as if nothing ever happened.

I lay down, stared at the ceiling for about thirteen seconds, and fighting back tears, entered my dreams willingly. They would attempt to make me feel better and hurt me at the same time. I was their pet. We always are.


I can't sleep.

I roll back over on my right side, take a sight or two of the darkness, and try to go back to head. It's too hot in here. My mind wanders. I think of that horrible kiss. I think of everything in the world that has hurt me, and why I haven't learned my lesson on avoiding it somehow. You would have thought some sort of shield would have been invented to fend off that kind of shit. But blankets and pillows can only go so far – the comfort of a room or a bed only can take you to a certain point before you have to make that leap yourself. Memories flood, I'm about to drown. No one to stop or save me. I'm not asking for help, though. I've been accustomed to doing this part alone, on my own. It's way too hot in this room. The door might get kicked in or the window might break; my mind is starting to make paranoid assumptions. Phone calls from the police; she sliced her wrists open with a steak knife or a box cutter, I have to go through the house and find other ripped things or other pieces of domestic memorabilia that I don't want have anything to do with. A wedding band, her old clothes, whatever it may be. My mind is racing. There's no water around in this room for me to drink; I have to get up if I want something. I don't want to face the cold, I don't want to face the heat, my mind is starting to wander and I'm starting to go a little crazy, my heartbeat is racing, my pulse is going through the roof, something, someone, calm me down, I'm on an edge of a moment that only visits me when I'm about to fall. I'm just seconds away from taking up a new habit just to forget the ones that I have; I'm back to hating air again, I'm back to doing something that I regret doing, I need to move.

I turn over and I try to fumble for the light, but give up before I fall out. I'm sweating and I'm thirsty. Cars rumble past and not one of them stop; I'm grateful because then I think they're there for me, to watch me leave or something. I hugged myself as I tried to figure out what was wrong with me. I was old enough to distinguish one disorder from another. I was old enough to get over this shit and just pass it off as teenage angst or depression or whatever. But here I was, alone, pretending that something was coming for me. I have problems. Please know this. I do and it's not anyone else's fault but mine. But I'm a shallow fucking wreck and I can't blame myself. Maybe my parents, maybe my mother. Or my father. Maybe it was all me. We all live on a minefield. We're not doctors and we're not gods, we're not better than anyone else, we're just destined to be people who can go from sweet to sour from bad to good in a moment's notice. What am I right now? I have a name, but I can't tell you anything good about it. It doesn't say anything about me. The only thing that speaks for me right now is my fear. Things are very weird right now and I'm trying to be very serious about all of this, but please know that I acknowledge the fact I have a lot of problems, and I'm doing the best I can to fix them. Just go with the flow. Accept these words and nightmares, and pretend that they're being said for a reason instead of just an idiotic shout in the dark to no one at all. All I do is just stand in the doorway, watching the red digital numbers die and change. I'm tempted to unplug the clock just so I don't have to watch it anymore. I close my eyes just to see the little color dots jump and bounce around like flies. Then, I hear a sound. I walk out into the living room and I wait. I continue to hug myself because there's no one else around.

She was never always like that. She had loved me in the beginning. She worshipped the idea of a marriage and I went with it because I was in love. That's always how it begins – with pure blindness, flowers, and friends that surround you in support because they're too weak-spined to tell you the truth about the girl. You go through the motions and begin to sense flat lines the very minute you tied the knot, but you ignore it because you're drunk, or you're having sex, and you want so desperately to believe that there is power in her eyes, or love in her skin, and you move along with the curves of her body, and you go so deep within her that it's all so real, that nothing could ever be a dream anymore, that reality has crushed fantasy so easily that the most inexpressible is the most realistic, but you wake up the next morning and think that you just committed yourself to the one person who could kill you the fastest and the most silently. But she was not like that – at first. She looked at me with those open brown eyes and held my hand at dinner and stressed to me that college was not the greatest thing in the world, but love – and the skin of a lover, and the hands of a man who would hold her and lift her up even if she was drowning on land, and I had proved to her, apparently, in the time that I had known her, that I was the person that could save her shaky soul and give her some sense to live, even if her family and her career did not.

So I saved her. I kissed her in the wind, I walked through her the snow, and I put every adventure I invented on hold so I could be with her in the cold and dull dark: I gave myself when I was at a time where I could not give myself. I was minutes away from going out into the real world and not being coddled anymore with this education shit, and yet, despite that numbing fear, I sacrificed my heart so she could have it. And for a while, she loved it. I was the only person she could confide in, even though she claimed she had friends, even though she claimed she had her art to fall back on – at the weakest parts of the day, she came to me, and she talked and whispered and shouted about all the bullshit in the world – but she did it to me, and for that, I bled out my own anger and absorbed hers. And the fucking beauty of it all is that I didn't mind. I wanted it. I thrived on it. It became my water. It became the bed I slept on and the rock I leaned up against. She had, in a sense, become born again through me, and I loved her for it. She had the most beautiful hair, the most beautiful eyes. I loved everything about her name, her slender body – I memorized how she would shower, I memorized how she ignored her previous boyfriends. I became obsessed with the fact that she wanted nothing but my mind to match hers when we lay in bed, and not once, did she ever, even think about breaking my heart.

But of course, things change fast, and luck always runs out. Dreams; they're always dead, they always die. Always.

She decided I wasn't good enough. She wanted to travel. She wanted to do these things for herself instead of us. And she also decided that she didn't want me to be by her side whenever she would. She felt ashamed to have me, to own me. In a sense, she wanted her heart back. I was, for all intents and purposes, a useless asshole.

That's how it always goes. Isn't it?

You admire their beauty. You watch in awe as they eat the shit that people give them, you love the way they do their hair, the clothes they dress in. You wonder how soft their skin is, you wonder how they do the artwork they do, you wonder if the name they really have is the name that really suits them. It's like you love them so much you want to be their creator even though they compliment you in so many other ways. Despite them being the one by your side, you put them on such a higher, holier ground: you give them the benefit of the doubt constantly and you wish that they loved you to the point where they wanted to be your creator, too. It's a chess game, a game of politics, and you wish it lasts forever.

Then they turn away from you.

And suddenly, it's no longer about admiring names or doing the right thing. It's all about how they feel about something that was so concrete. In the months I loved her, the love was so concrete and for real: but it only was real because there was no feeling, it just WAS. The beauty of the beauty in the relationship is that you don't think about any of it – you act upon your instinct, and you give it your all without saying a fucking word. Always. You let the heart decide, and you never, not once, consider that feelings and reasoning is allowed for any second. It's almost as if thought – the one thing that a higher being granted us, even though it wanted for us to stay inferior – becomes the new boyfriend or the new lover or even the new place that lovers go to escape old, boring ones. Which has become me, which has become her – which has become all of us, at one point, whether we admit it or not.

I'm just trying to put into words the shallowness of both me and her. I'm not saying I'm a model example of what love should be. I'm merely trying to figure out as to why she did what she did, and why I did what I did, only with more feeling, with more memory. In a sense, I would love for the past to be the fucking past and let bygones be bygones. But not this time. There's too much darkness in my eyes and too much pain in my heart to let rust overtake us. It's a thirst I'd like to have quenched. Why she – once an admirable beauty – now suddenly becomes the shallow hole in a field that's supposed to be flat.

I'm sure all of this now is a story no one wants to touch or be a part of. It's evil and envious and full of loss and sorrow and all of that shit. But what it has that no one will admit is truth. I'm not seeking to point out the flaws in the human race. I'm merely asking that all of us, past our tired eyes and hands, that we have this different idea of love, that we embody specific qualities, and that no one ever matches up perfectly except the few and the promising. Those are the people that we never see because they believe the universe spins, is positive and is the basis for them and only them. But for the rest of us, who believe in dark hearts and still portraits of Earth, we wind up being the nameless and the void-fillers: all of our kind exists on our streets, and even though I did her the largest favor in the world by leaving her, she gave herself the biggest scar on her skin if she thought she was going to have me, love me, unlove me, and think she was going to fucking get away with it.

I fight back.

And this time, I'm fighting to win.

And it's time her name is said without any honor attached to it. I feel like she lost that right, and if we're playing for points, then neither does mine. But at least I died doing the right thing, and she died by simply being useful and valuable to no one in particular.


It's only fair to show you more of her mind, at least, the few fragments I saw and understood. When we were together, I had felt I was being judged for even speaking. Towards the end, I almost wrote down everything I would say to her on paper. She didn't like it whenever I would have an occasional drink. She never liked it when one of my friends called because I would be gone for hours. I know none of this sounds mature or any of my reasons seem justified, but I'll do a little exercise for you and then you'll understand. Count all the windows and doors in your house. If they are less than the amount of times that she belittled you in public or outright told you that you were stupid, then you'll see what I mean.

It's like knowing you have no heart. It's like feeling blood in parts of your body that they're not supposed to go to, like the eyes or the mouth. She brought that feeling to me; a feeling that I thought would never hit me. She could make crowded rooms empty when she put her thoughts to words. A troubling thing, I know, but it more or less describes her frozen nature: she was erratic, dumbfounded by simple things, and when it came to my declarations of love, they were nothing more than random lines of poetry scattered on the air of the world. It's why I don't like to breathe it sometimes: I know her existence has tainted it.

A lot of her words and her dreams have made me question what exactly serenity really is. It made me question if muscles really do have the power to relax, and if sleep really is a break from the real world. A lot of her personality depends on whether or not you're good enough for her that she should keep you as a friend or not. All of what she ever wanted to do relied on her ability to zone things out, such as people or beauty or even love, and she never really got into the whole idea of feeling so connected to someone that she couldn't get close enough to them. Many times I would think sleeping with her was just something to do instead of something we wanted to do. Rarely did she run her hand over my skin, or even made a sexual comment that got me aroused. Sexuality, as it seemed, was still a foreign definition. But it's not important enough to be mentioned further. It was just an example of the things she would do. I don't want to say she was a robot, but her face lacked smiles, and her hands lacked adventure, at least, the adventure that we used to agree upon when we were young. Communication became as silent as the wind over the trees in the woods.

Of course, not all of her has made me who I am now. I have my problems, too, as we have discovered. There's anger and there's swarms of emotions that I never thought I had before or the falling snow, or driving my car into the snow, or even throwing rocks at loved ones in the playground. It's a fear that has been in me, I suppose, ever since my parents have gotten together. It's the stress of realizing that one day you might be like them, and you grow up trying to decide if you can avoid it, or if there's things you should do to be like them in the hopes that it would make them happy, but even then, you just go crazy with the thought that no matter how much you drink and how much you pretend and how much love you put into someone, you come to the sad conclusion that nothing makes you happy, not even the planet, and the only thing you're in debt to is nightmares, because they make you realize just how fucking amazing the dream world is. For anyone who is in that dream world, or has ever experienced it, keep it. Don't let anyone talk you out of it.

People will do this to you. If you're not bitter or enraged by the time you grow up, then you have nothing to show for it. Any and all art is based on this, and love is founded on these principles as well. If you can't abuse others and lie to them, then you might as well not even love. She had this down to a science, and now she gave it to me. The writing was on the wall, and even before the paint on the canvas was dry, she showed me what it was like to love someone wholeheartedly, then broken, and then paralyzed and speechless. It was as if an experiment to capture daylight was only being attempted at midnight. Circles become vicious cycles, words of love become whispers to ignore. The color of her hair becomes the color of hair you hate the fucking most. You never again want to hear the word softness. You get sick at the thought of bare skin. You do anything in your power to avoid driving down their street. All in all, you'd rather take a shadow and just place it over that part of your life, and hope that if they never have an emergency, that they never call you for anything. That's the part of love that is now occupied by her. That's the part that wakes me up in the middle of night and wants me to drink it or smoke it away.

She was a ghost of a different nature. She was the kind of person who did not believe in the religion of favors or the concepts of purity. She was a void that only brought things to her benefit, and some people have asked me what I was thinking when I started to date her. To this day, I don't know. I was blown away by the outside and thought nothing of the inside. My answer is that I simply wasn't thinking, and her fragments, the ones that were flawed and crude, became the death of the relationship. Was it me, in the beginning? It may have been. Was it me, in the ending? Of course. I made the move to disappear. But there was a cold spot in the middle of this heat that she had flipped the switch, and from the end of the beginning to near the end – the spots where the timelines are blurry and vague – she had orchestrated clearly what was to me, the biggest heart attack of my life and the largest bout of depression and doubt that I could have ever seen. She was a demon. So was I. But two demons in the same room eventually have to disperse, because there's a bigger evil to lay claim to. And I decided to find it. She merely fell into herself and decided I wasn't one to be worshipped.

What it boils down to his shame. And it can never be presented as something else. Love becomes a game, and the broken hearts lose, and everything else wins.

We're designed to kill. Even in seclusion and passion. The hands that love become the strongest weapons. We don't ever want to admit it, but sometimes when we lie in bed, dreaming about things, holding the person you love, you think for very brief moments what it would be like to just be superior. To be the winner. I don't mean death. Or torture. I just mean moments where you both wake up in the morning and even know you had an argument the night before and you think you're wrong, that she'll miraculously wake up and just submit to you. Give to you. Make you be the better person in every way. It's things like this that lovers don't want to do because they don't like to think it. They think love is all flowers and poetry and happiness. But it's more than that. I don't like to admit it. I don't want to think about love as a bad thing, because when it works, it works. It's a beautiful thing where white light is all that exists. But when she walks away from you, and goes to someone else as quick as that, it leaves you standing in a room, by yourself, hugging yourself, because your arms once touched hers, and it makes you happy. Briefly.

I'm watching the world stay dark outside my window. I'm almost afraid to go to sleep because I have no clue how she or anything else is going to get the best of me tonight. Something once safe has the highest power to hinder, hurt and defile. It's not so much how my heart handles these dreams. It's the lack of respect that my heart has for my head, to put it through that shit. It's amazing how the body can heal as quickly as it can attack. It's just one of those thoughts that become more real and destructive with every second, every breath, every droplet of time that threatens our human fabric. And when I do fall asleep, I do see her come towards me, and she's almost always in her wedding dress. She becomes the most beautiful thing my mind can conjure. She's of pure validity, brute strength. I dream of the ways I will have sex with her that night, how I will undress her beauty and find another one hiding underneath, of which I'll take copious notes so I can use them for my benefit when I'm alone, when she's somewhere else, unable to take me into her. And she's whispering a language of love into her bouquet of flowers, through her veil, through the vows she wrote the months beforehand as mine I wrote only days before, and before she takes my name for all eternity, and promises to take care of me, she turns into darkness visible, a shadow, a fire that knows no home but an asylum full of friends that will help it burn. And she wants nothing else but for me to disappear. And I try to stop her but she goes to kiss and I know it's not a kiss but an attack, a weapon. And I wake up in cold sweats, I wake up in shivers, and when I go to call her, I forget the number, I forget the house, and I think, she may be doing the same exact thing, her body wracked with the cries and the tears she wished she would never have, and she goes to call me, and she has no idea where I am. The nightmare I put her is strong enough to kill me. She has no clue where I am, but I know where she is, and I wind up fucking laughing at her. God. There is something wrong with me. There is something, truly, honestly wrong with me. To think of love this way. To do this to someone I respect. To be able to go to our house and treat her like that.

It's almost like I handed her the gun. Like I supplied the bullet, sharpened the blade, taped up the only hole in which to escape.

I have fallen. I have become like a pendant fallen from someone's neck. I have become something like a sneaking glance, like a star whistling through trees in a barren homeland. I'm everything and nothing. I have fallen just like her and possibly you and we meet here at this winding road. I am sorry for what I am going to do to you and her. I am unlike any other person you will ever meet again, and I wish deep down that I had nothing but good graces to give you. I'm many things at once, a hybrid that still breathes air but does not wish to have any other source of energy. Maybe except blood. A soul. Memory. The taste of something else. I'm really sorry. I wish I could explain it better. Maybe when everyone reads this after I die they'll piece it together. Forensic experts always do. But I've never done this before, so you tell me what will happen. I will almost guarantee you're smarter than me, so if you go on a search of my possessions after I die, and if you find this, give it to someone who will help other people like me. Make copies, and then burn this. I don't want my handwriting to be seen by any copycats or protestors. I want to be unique, a rebel. But only in my own head. I don't want this to lead to death, if I see you or anyone else. I just really want a friend. I don't mean to sound like this. I should write like I was earlier, cathartic, dense, vague and friendly. I don't want to sound like them. I didn't want to fall. But I was, and still am, and someone has to fucking come with me. It just has to be this way. It's unfortunate, but it's not like more are being born every day. And they'll learn to appreciate what they have, after they see what will happen tonight. God help me, forever, and now, at the time of my collapse.

I have to get it together. Talking like this isn't helping anybody at all.

I deserve to get murdered in my sleep. Maybe next time she comes toward me in that wedding dress, I'll let her sink her beautiful teeth in my rotten neck, and my skin will peel like an old peach, and everything in me will fall to the ground and just withdraw into a filthy spot. I make my way back to the bed, in my casket. I'm covered in sweat and regret. I'm only thinking of words in the air, her wedding dress, and what she did after I left.

It's probably better that I can't picture it.


I did have a dream of her that night. I knew I would. It went like this:

I dreamed that I was dead, and when I found out, I actually laughed. I was ruined instead of her, and soul lived without body, and I floated above her, in the sky, like some sort of demented being, watching over her, trying to give her my voice, and it was a waste of time. So, I became a ghost of the bright blue afternoon sky, and I would ride above her and watch her on Earth, like I was on a zip line, following her where she went. And I would talk to her and try to tell her things, what the afterlife was, but she could not hear me, naturally. She was heartbroken, devastated, didn't eat right, didn't flirt, just wasn't herself. And I would scream at her at different intervals in this dream to just look up, I was right there, right fucking there, all she had to do was look up at the stars and I would make everything all right again, I would be a much better husband and that I was sorry for everything I did to her. I just wanted her to look up so she would see me, and hopefully, not start running.

But she would never do it, and her days became meaningless and my days became meaningless. After a while, I caught on to the horror of this, and I tried in vain to wake up, but it was all for naught. My brain really wanted me, I know, to sit through this and really experience what was going on; insanity was rearing its ugly head again, smiling for everyone to see. and then at one point in the dream, I was watching her from up top of our old apartment building, and she was walking through a park with another man. I couldn't see who he was, and for whatever reason, I became frozen at one fixed point, unable to move at all to get a face, and she was trying not to hold hands or laugh at this person's joke, but she was starting to slip, starting to accept that being with someone else was ok after a certain period of time, and I was screaming her name at the top of my dead lungs, begging her not to do it, and she never did. She went into the opposite direction after a while, and my heart had been beating so fast it was a wonder I was even dead.

And the dream felt like weeks and weeks long, as I watched her progress slowly with this newfound grief: I watched her write down his name a thousand times like she admitted she did. She would go through my things, keep what she wanted, donate all the rest, and she would wear my clothes to work, as all of her friends slowly distanced themselves from her, saying, that fucking girl, why doesn't she just move on? why is she loving someone that isn't here? and I stood right by her, trying to touch her on her slender shoulders and say, just join me, just come with me, and we'll be alright. We don't have to worry about a thing anymore. But she never would. I would tell her as best as I could to forgive me, that all was much better here in death, and we wouldn't have to live life by constricting standards anymore. But, just like she was in life, she would not listen. And I continued to look like the asshole.

And the dream ended with a horrific image I would never be able to forget: it had been years later, and one tragedy after another occurred, and she had wound up at the ocean by herself. I watched her from the clouds as the saltwater sprayed all over her body, making her cold. She watched the seagulls fly through the air but was still unable to see my spirit. She had brought some sort of bag with her, and she opened the bag, and pulled out a raft. She had filled up the raft as best as she could, and she laid on it, and drifted off into the sea, hands on her shoulders, crossed, as if she was performing her own funeral. And she was crying the loss of love, the feeling of happiness, as she began calling for her own death, for some sort of storm or wave to carry her away into this nothingness, to end these years where she would constantly have to relive her love through daydreams and my old clothes and things, and I was yelling at her until murky blood came out of my mouth, to turn back and start over, that it was ok, it was ok, and she kept floating, muttering to herself like someone who just had nothing left, and I crashed into the water, disrupting the flow of my ethereal state, as I tried to push her back to dry land, but she would have none of it. I could smell her so clearly even in the dream, and eventually, I gave up, accepting death, accepting the dark blue and gray ending of this sea that was to drown our souls. So I climbed next to her on the raft, just enough room for both, and I whispered to her, i'm here now, it's ok, it's all ok, and she would just keep talking, as if she was giving a eulogy, or writing a book, or maybe comforting herself with the only blanket she had since my arms died along with the rest of my body. and then, just as

I went to kiss her on the cheek and ride off together, I woke up.

I twitched awake and laid there until the sweat stopped rolling off my face. I could only lay there. I had no idea what it meant. But the scariest feeling of it all is that I came to a conclusion that I didn't want to have.

I still loved her. And I still want to talk about her to you.

I know that I jump around a lot when I talk about her. One moment, I about want to strangle her, and then the next, I'm defending her, praising her. I wonder why I do that. I think it has to do with time. Theorists and philosophers give time many different meanings, and I think it's because of its diversity that it ruins us. I mean, some people say it heals all, and some people say it makes your pain worse. But what do I know about time? Time and all of its idiotic persuasion. What it can do to the human spirit. Lifeless, tasteless, odorless, yet so dominant and realistic. Sharp like a scalpel, silent as snow. Maybe it is the master, the God of the world. The new breath of life into a seemingly careless entity. It is time that makes all of these decisions for us, and ruins them too. How bright it is, how utterly, perpetually light it is, and yet, there is loveless dark with it, a virtual shape of death and quiet hovering above, waiting, stalking, unwearyingly, tolerant of humans, casually remarking of their downfall and waiting to smash the remains into stoic, pleading pieces. Funny how people are so young and they realize is when they are brought up in safety bubbles and nets, waiting for the world to pass them by so they can go back to their toys. But some people cannot hide from it. They are designated from birth to be targets. It's not the person's fault. It just happens that way. It more or less just gives some people a reason to be angry, a reason to smash up their own homes and faces in their private times. They want to complain about it but they do not want to sound whiny or selfish, they just hold it in until the ire can no longer stay within its room. It gets curious and wants to crawl, just like a baby. And then it takes on a mind of its own. Why? Because of time. It all goes back to this.

This is what happens when she wakes me up. I get like this. And I know I mind it, but tonight I don't think it bothers me as much as a normal night. Because tonight, with her, was not normal. It was definitely wrong. And precious. So many opposites, converging, like cars coming up on a curve with no guardrail to hold them back.

I get out of bed and go to the bathroom. I sit there for a minute to collect my thoughts, see where they want to go, see where I want them to go, see how they defy me.

I've lost control of them so I let my mind wander. Seeing her in my sleep brings back a lot of feeling, a certain fire I don't necessarily want to have lit right now, because it's late enough to know that I should be sleeping, and that a new day is going to dawn, and I don't want to start it off with feeling her again. And by feeling her I mean that seeing her in all those poses today, those outfits, those curves and her hair, her skin laughing at me, her hands lonely and unaccustomed to dull and ache, all of that is starting to come together into a moment that I don't want to share with myself, because it'll only be me doing it, and it'll only be a temporary fix to what I really need to do: forget. but it'll worsen it, intensify it, and then just as I go to sit up and go back to bed, and try again, I think of how her body was in that water, lightly caressing the ocean's breast, and before I know it, I'm doing what I have to do to get my mind to shut the fuck up.

Pride has nothing to do with it. It just is what it is.

I might as well go to one of my favorite times with her to get this over with the fastest way possible. I don't think of it so much as just us doing a normal sexual thing, and when I do, I feel like an animal, so I'm going to pretty up the memory just well enough for me to pass this off as lust instead of love:

*Her body, a figure of light. Wrapped around me like colors on a fantastic, perfect sight. There was no dullness to her windswept hair, her rain-covered face. Eyes and glances like razors digging into fruit, hands as relaxing as anything, resting on my leg. A giggle escaped from her throat when I told her a dirty joke and then she playfully slapped me. "Don't ever tell a lady something like that", she would say right after. We're sitting and watching the river overrun in the woods, walking and standing on rocks, talking about what we would do when we would become older. Would we stay lovers, would we believe in love, would we even stay talking to each other? I said yes, all the time. We would stop and sit on a rotten oak, leaves like nothing, branches as frail as the whispers of other lovers they knew. "They're so fake, they're so fucking unbelievably fake," she would say as she took her slender legs and straddled me as we sat on the log, her hands on my shoulders, lips a hairsbreadth away from connecting and destroying the boundaries of public attention. I wished so badly we were older, that we were married (we had just started dating) and having kids, to show them all that love could win and would overcome any obstacle. She would put a finger to my lips and say, "Don't spoil the moment. We're not here to talk about the future. We're just here to plan it in our heads and talk about now. don't rush things". But I would say to her, in my mind, what about passion? You run right through me, your beauty breaks through any sky or yard, cold or hot, gray or white, you flatten any evil thought I ever think about, the clarity of your structure is enough to bust me wide open and forget what I ever learned about motor skills, logic, learning, mathematics, linguistics, I forget what sound even sounds like when I hear you speak, because you break the barrier, you have burned the mold, you bring safety in numbers, you are the universe, the system, the flame, all of what remained from drawings and engineering you are the result of perfectly organized love. Why can't I say I want to marry you? Why don't you want to think about all the possibilities? And she would finally kiss me as the rain encircled them, and I would say, oh yes. because there are a million things to explore first. And the current situation, you on top of me, requires strict attention. We fall on the forest floor and forgot about what we needed to do in the real life.*

*"Take me," she proclaims.*

*Into the atmosphere, memoirs of past love burn away into the silence. Ghosts of men who have hurt her will and pierced her skin with lies; into the depths of her long auburn strands of hair contains previous fingerprints of men who made false promises and accusations, threatening to be violent to her if love was not fulfilled to their own sick degree. They start to fade into the fire around them where they get swallowed by a creature who proclaims nothing but sacred love.*

*But it doesn't matter now, as our lips linger in mid-air on the ground. And shadows of two lovers in solitude are painted onto the wall of nature, silhouettes signifying no sound whatsoever. Our skin alone makes warmth, enough fire for two hundred thousand gasps of life.*

*Quickly, in one fluid motion, she lies on top of him, chests meeting and becoming a creation, and their hearts their hearts beat together, and she goes to cry out of perfection.*

*She falls victim to my touch, and she positions her sacred body next to mine, skin together, and I lay my hand on her shoulder. Loosely her hair tumbles onto my chest, but I pay no mind to it, and allow it to sway in a sea of beauty, and she goes to sleep in my arms. In all of these woods, we hear sounds until we breathe straight into dreams.*

I snap out of it, clean up. Like I said, it is what it is. I didn't want to do it, I immediately regret it, just because I need to deprive myself of times like those. Why? Because they are never, ever coming back, and there is no point to it all. I can't torture myself like that, thinking that tomorrow she'll call and want me back, and everything will be alright. There will be plenty of twists and turns and we think we can do it, and then we won't be able to. It's just the end, and there's nothing I can do. I turn off the light, and feeling weaker and more pathetic, I try this thing called sleep again, see where it takes me now.

When I finally do pass out, I get this memory:

*She appears at my work one day. She's in a blue sundress, her hair in braids. She's wearing the whitest shoes I've ever seen. And she's all smiles. I can feel the angel in her without her even addressing me. I can just get comfortable knowing that her light is near mine. She comes up to my cubicle. How she did this I'll never know. It's best that the story has its plot holes. Otherwise it wouldn't be love. It'd be something else.*

*"You look beautiful," I said to her. The first words out of my mouth, usually ninety nine percent of the time. It was practiced, but by that point, automatic.*

*She smiled a million dollar smile. She was up to something, usually no good. But this was about a month or so after we got married, and this was still the honeymoon era. As short and confusing as it was.*

"Well, hello, baby," she said, leaning over to give me a kiss on the cheek. She pulled away and I felt the lipstick marking me. She never wore lipstick. Definitely something was up.

"Well, hi. You found me. How did you get past security?"

"Sir," she said, sitting in the empty chair next to my desk, "there are just some things that are meant to stay unanswered."

"Like what?"

"The universe."

"What else?"

"Why you can drive on parkways and park on driveways. Why you play at a recital and recite at a play. Why the Mariners have never been to the World Series. Why they put leeches on Lord Byron. Things like that."

"So you're telling me," I said, taking off my glasses and putting down my pen, "that your reason for being here is comparable to those mysteries?"

She frowned, briefly. Her dimples flared, her hair shone, her eyes bulged wide with anticipation. She knew how to work her body. "Well, for a little while. Of course you'll figure it out and the fun will be ruined. But for now, yes, I guess I can say that, sure."

I smiled. "You know, you could get a job here. Talking in circles. You'd be perfect management. Half of what you say never makes sense. You'd be a natural fit."

She put on a mock-insulted face. "Now, what a horrible thing to say to your wife!"

"How about I say something nice to win back her love?"

"Like what?"

"That she's a lovely lady and her smile does wonders."

"Not good enough."

"What about that she's a joy to wake up next to and a wonderful cuddler?"

"Close. But not quite good enough."

"How about that she's a fine cook."

"Ugh. Losing points, buddy. Going backwards."

"How about quite simply, that it is an honor and a privilege, to have your hand in mine, and to be my queen to my king, and that sleeping next to your fine naked body every night is something so wonderful that I should have to pay for it."

"You're saying i'm a prostitute!"

"Not quite. More like..."

"Oh, I'd love to hear this," she said, crossing her legs, showing me the smoothness and tan of them. I was *starting to lose my armor. She would want me to start making out with her in the middle of the office. It was a game we would play when we were out and about. Let's see what we can show these people of the world, if I can just flirt with him long enough.*

*I waved her off. "I love you."*

*She smiled that smile again. "I love you, too. That works for now. But as far as that whole sleeping next to me thing tonight..."*

*"I suppose I lost it. The king will have to sleep out in the bunkhouse with the goats."*

*"I reckon so."*

*"So," I said, "now that we cleared all that up, you must inform me, now, and not a minute to spare, why you came here, and what you had to tell me."*

*"It's a surprise," she started.*

*"How big?"*

*"Roughly an inch."*

*"Ok."*

*"And it's got some color to it."*

*"Can it sing?"*

*"No, not very well."*

*"Can it make me breakfast?"*

*"If you train it right."*

*"Will it be able to finish this assignment on time for me?"*

*"Not a chance. That's for mortals. This is something much wider in scope."*

*"Is it a moon bounce?"*

*"Now why would it be a moon bounce?"*

*"I've always wanted one."*

*"What are you, five?"*

*"Don't lie to me, babe. You've always wanted a moon bounce."*

*"Yeah, maybe when I was still beating the shit out of Ken with a crab hammer."*

*"What was your childhood like, not being able to enjoy certain things?"*

*"Like fucking moon bounces?"*

*"That, and Polly Pockets."*

*"I never played with Polly Pockets!"*

*"Ok, fine, Cabbage Patch dolls."*

*"Back to subject, mister."*

*"Glad you admitted it."*

*"Anyway, sir, it is not a moon bounce. And you're not going to get one, ever. This surprise is something that is much more wonderful. It is full of love. It is full of whimsy and magic and it's going to make us happy for a very long time. And I found it. And I want you to know that*

*I did everything in my power to make it happen. And I tried to keep it a secret as best as possible, and I think I have, because as you're looking at me with that dumb puppy dog look, I can see that you have no idea what it is, and that is why I'm smiling so big, and because I was so happy, I dressed in the prettiest way I could because good news deserves to be told by a wife who looks stunning enough to be a...I guess, as you put it, a queen. I like that much more now, thinking about it."*

*"So, what is it?"*

*She sighed heavily. "I have to show you. In person. Which means you have to come with me. Without thinking about it. Just come forward and I will show you the way."*

*I looked at the clock on the computer. "I have a meeting in a half hour. Can this surprise wait until maybe, 2 o'clock?"*

*She got off the chair and looked at me dead in the eyes. It was moments like this where I knew I would stay young, even when I knew I wouldn't. You ever have those conflicted emotions? Where you know you're going to have love forever, even when you're standing around her, unable to translate anything, unable to comprehend or understand what's going on? I had known, at this moment, that we were going to stay together forever even if we split up. I know that may be a weird thing to hear, especially in my own flashback, but I can remember it so clearly, like I fell directly into cold water, and the shock, the extreme sense of feeling, just etched itself into my mind easily, and that's why I'm able to recite everything so perfectly, even when I'm feeling so angry and upset towards her now. Because I see her, in this blue sundress, hair in braids, smooth legs. And she's on the verge of straddling me in the office, ready to take me into her, office etiquette be damned. I would have went with it if she did. But all I did at the time was just stare back at her. Her eyes, like dark pools. Things like that. Things that lovers say. Sometimes, I think I should have followed my writing a little more seriously. Because I can't love properly, and all I can do to her for you is talk about her, and it gives you the sense that maybe you know someone like her, or that you are her, and if you are, I'm sorry. Because the things you do to people just isn't right.*

*"Love does not wait, my pretty little king," she said, whispering to me, starting to untie my tie with her slender fingers. She brought her lips to my ear and gave a little bite. Then, in a sultry voice, she uttered, "and her majesty may want a little afternoon ceremony, if you shall so allow it."*

Shivers ran up and down my body. She had read my mind and delivered my next line.

"You'll be back before your meeting, I promise. It's just down the road. So don't get all uptight," she said, leaning back from me, showing me her full frame again. "I wasn't kidding about the session, though. The quicker you leave, the quicker you can come back. Take my hand. I have many perfect and indescribable things to bestow upon you, and you will love it with all your heart." She extended and once more, smiled. I couldn't resist.

"To hell with it all!" I bellowed, and she giggled. I got up off the chair and she led me out of the building. Down the hallways, I could feel the stares from my co-workers, and at the time, I was thinking to myself, they are so jealous. They just have no clue how great my life is. But now, I laugh to myself. They were probably saying shit about me, and I know, deep down, it wasn't good for me. They were one hundred percent correct about me. I was living a nonlife with a woman that wasn't going to stay very long. Something bad was going to happen. Little did they know how bad it got. They'll never know. That's why strangers are so kind and wonderful. They're clueless and they're harmless.

When we got outside, we were met with a downpour. Rain fell like dreams as it pounded the street and started to flood the walkways. People were running to and fro with suitcases and umbrellas and cars honked horns incessantly in an effort to be heard instead of seen. The trees danced in the wind and I stopped her just as we were turning the corner.

"So you're going to give me my death of cold, eh?"

"Oh, stop it," she said, as water covered every inch of her. She wiped it out of her eyes. "I didn't know it was going to rain. It was sunny as hell when I got here."

I looked down at my shirt and pants, all soaked, and not a change of clothes in the office. "Well, I guess they're just going to have to accept my proposal, despite the fact that I hit a water buffalo."

Without a word, we took hands and walked down the city street. We were the only ones moving at our own pace. And I guess what makes this memory so peaceful and breathtaking - and for other reasons that my subconscious just won't admit right now - is that I remember how calm we both were, and we didn't even have to say anything to each other on how to act. It was just a natural behavior not to worry about the storm. We knew we were going to be soaked no matter what, so what was the rush? Why do people run around acting like it's the end of the world? The day goes on, the clock ticks. I guess some people just are so stressed that they won't allow things like this to happen. They're all going to die angry and miss everything cool that this world has to offer. As we walked past storefronts, markets, and apartment buildings, there were a few like us, watching the rain, absorbing the situation, not worrying about anything other than their own moments, which was relaxing enough for me to walk with my wife in the middle of what turned out to be a nondescript day - except for what she had to show me, something strong enough to make me pull it out of my head even when I sleep.

"How far away is this surprise?"

"A hop, a skip, and a jump away," she said as she opened her mouth to catch the raindrops and drink them down.

"Don't drink that, there's bad stuff in there."

"It's water!"

"Yeah, but there's bad chemicals in there. Atmosphere junk."

"God, you are so lame," she laughed. "And so full of shit."

"So can this surprise speak? Can it say words?"

"Of course. Just not full sentences. Why, do you want everything explained to you in this life?"

That turned out to be one of the more prophetic statements of our whole relationship.

"What else can it do?"

"Can't you just wait? We're almost there."

"Sure thing."

I squeezed her hand tighter. I was enjoying the hell out of this, more than I thought I ever would. I took my cell phone out of my pocket with my other hand and dialed the department secretary. I told her (and I had been searching far and wide for an opportunity to use this excuse, and I was in a good mood, so forgive me if this sounds a little gross) that I had come down with a bad case of anal glaucoma, as in 'I just didn't see my ass coming back in today'. When I hung up the phone, she roared in delight.

"Where did you hear that from?"

"An old friend. I was always on the edge with using it before, but I figure now was the best time to do it."

"For reasons unbeknownst to me now, I love you more than I did fifteen minutes ago."

"You should write all these things you say down, babe. Say them to our kids years down the road."

She stopped briefly to look at me. The rain was coming down so heavy we couldn't see all the little details of our faces, just the big picture. I could see that her *braids were undone, that her smile turned to a curious sulk, like I had just offended her in the worst way. This is where if I wanted a nightmare to ever turn to, I would go to this still image right here. All of this is still a movie that I'm creating for you, and I hope you see it as such, because this is where the tension goes to rebuild. She stood silent for a minute, then quietly spoke.*

*"What did you say?"*

*"Did I say something wrong?"*

*"I asked you what you said."*

*"I said to say these things to our kids years down the road."*

*"That's what I thought you said," she said, and she dropped her head.*

*"Why, what's wrong with that?"*

*It took her some time before she lifted her head up again. This is still when I wanted to fight for love, tooth and nail, and I wanted to take her in my arms and profusely apologize. But instead, I could see that she was doing this weird smiling-laughing thing, and I pushed the rainwater out of her eyes with my thumb and went to kiss her. As I did, she took it half-heartedly, and just put her hand on my cheek.*

*I said her name. "What's wrong?"*

*"I just wish you could see the difference between the rain and my tears. Because I'm crying right now."*

*"I'm sorry if I upset you."*

*"No, no, it's happiness."* And she wrapped her arms around my waist. *"I never thought we would get to this point. To be able to say it so casually and to mean it. You honestly see having kids with me?"*

*At the time, I did. Now, not so much. I'll be lucky if I ever get to that point with anyone else again. But like anybody else in a situation like this, I wanted so badly to make it true. Because I felt it. And love does these things to you. Love is a better religion or cult that Christianity or Catholicism or Buddhism or whatever the fuck you believe in. Love makes you make insane decisions and makes you kill men and gives you faith more purer than anything else ever put together. It just does. I once believed that the heart was just a muscle, that it pumped blood and kept you alive and nothing else. That it did not feel love, but you only just thought it made love, and that love was only in your head. I had a girl once, before her, that said she loved me with all her mind and nothing else. Well, that's fucking bullshit. There's a reason why she's no longer in my life. Because love is too strong of a thing to be felt with just your mind. Your brain is the biggest liar of them all. So how could you trust that judgment at all? So ever since then - at least, the time I was with her - I learned to go with my heart, and then, when she asked me that question, I wanted it badly. So I told her the truth.*

*"Yes. I want kids with you," I said. I expected her to interrupt but when she didn't, I continued. "I want everything with you. I want to wake up and stay young and watch you grow old with me. I want to see sunrises and sunsets in different countries and different states and be able to watch you grow as a person. I want to see your dreams go with mine and start new beginnings and end the old endings that still trouble you. I want to be able to tell jokes and go with you to places that normally wouldn't have us. I want to have children with you and teach them the things that our parents couldn't teach us and I want to be a good influence on them just as much as you so they can grow into adults and be as creative and practical as us. I want all of those things the minute I said yes on the altar with you. Truth is, I could never tell this to anyone before, not even in false hopes or as a joke. I just want these things with you. You doing things like this only confirms it. I want to be able to have my son or my daughter look at you and be proud that they can call you their mother. I want that for you, and I want that for us. And I want to be able to do that now. I don't want to wait. I want it to be real, and I want it to be now. Right now. No*

*sense in waiting. No sense in hiding it and not planning for the future. Let's plan for the future right now. Let's do it today. Let's already get tomorrow done with. Let's do what we can."*

*So easy, this lie. I never spoke that fast, that hard, that passionate before in my life. It was like I was an actor. And my tongue did not fail me. I spoke gracefully, without taking a breath, without stopping to fact check or trip over a fallacy. It was an adventure in speech, and a language professor would be proud of me. Although I'm sure a theorist would tear me apart.*

*She looked at me with power I never saw before. I'm sure that she was searching deep in her feminine soul, trying to decipher what I was saying, running it through translation services, asking herself the age-old question: 'is he fucking with me?' She put her hand in front of her face again, to hold back the behemoth-sized sob I'm sure she was building in her throat. I held her in the rain. She started to shake. For a minute, I was worried that it was not the right time. But it FELT like the right time. Isn't that what love is about? Saying what you need to say? Regardless of whether it's the right time or not. How does my mind come up with these questions only when I sleep? Why can't I have the real answers? Why does it always have to be a fight?*

*Why does someone always have to lose?*

*I let her go after a few seconds. She pulled me back in again. There I go again, ruining the moment. How was I supposed to know?*

*I kneeled down a little more, so that she was face to face with me. I put my lips to her ear. I started to whisper to her. This is where my mind begins to fail. Maybe I'm waking up. Maybe I'm starting to realize that I am just not meant to remember anything, as a way of my mind going 'you fucked up, you can't start over, it's just not meant to be.' I tried as best as I could to fix the beauty. But what about beauty? Isn't it just a phase? Can't you choose when to be ugly, when to be beautiful? Are you born with it? I wasn't. Not by a long shot. Affection does not go with me. I was meant to suffer. I guess I must be pretty fucked up as a person if I want, or rather, desire, to push affection away.*

*"It's ok, it's ok," I kept saying. I didn't know what else to do.*

*She let go of me again after a few seconds. She spoke as the rain fell into her mouth, but she did not want to drink it.*

*"What are you thinking?"*

*After some time, she began to speak, but very broken, very quietly.*

*"I don't think I want to show you the surprise anymore."*

*So much for civility. So much for the ever-proud domestic life. So much for the chance to be able to remember what the fuck any of this was.*

I woke up nervous. Cold sweat. Shaking bones, dead weight, open mouth, nothing around like water to have. Just darkness. Enough darkness to try to swallow, and eventually, choke on. I knew what I did and it made me feel sick. In the bathroom before I slept. I know what I did and I shouldn't have because it made me care about her again, care in a different way. Almost like affection, that I should fight for her, like I did the night at the bar when I almost lost my hand. It was an old noise tuned up to a different frequency, new pitch, new layers, a soundscape for the painfully obvious, a song to fan the flames of disconnection and discontent. But was it losing her, that fear that drove me to that feeling to fight? Was it love for her or a need to save myself? That whole dream, seeing her again - I was left freezing, wanting to attach myself to bare skin again, specifically hers. But is that lust? Love? Or is it just the loneliness? The dress, the braids, the rain, the prayer and hope that we would have kids, that I would enter her to begin life and then just as soon as I promise to, I leave? What was it?

I sat up, looked at the clock. It was almost time to get up for work anyway.

Dreams. What the hell are they? What do they do?

Every time these things happen, I engage in these fantasies and the same few things always come up, like clockwork - I wind up being guilty, I'm afraid of being irrational and immature, I celebrate the insignificant things just to please myself and only to hurt her, just because I'm afraid to accept her happiness, that I have to ruin it with what I want and don't even consider the fact that she would want the opposite, and then when I would finish, I just store it away and I'm unable to go back to how it was. I go back to what only I want to, and because I only see my side, I hate myself, and I hate her for not stopping me. Not stopping my maniacal ways, not stopping me from taking over her. Why? My mind destroys normal feelings, like the final line of that dream. The domestic disappears, the circle splits open like morning, the night comes and doesn't want to go. And then her skin fades, as does her clothes and her impact on this planet, and then she's just another lover lost in the annals of this terrible world.

And once I do that, I have to start over, all over - with making promises to another girl, going through the bullshit of meeting the parents and retreading ground by sharing secrets and likes and dislikes, and every time I think of myself going through those moments with other women again, I sit there and stop myself because no one could do it like her, so why even try, why even start over? I might as well just accept the fact that she's the only lover in the world. And if she has to exist superficially in my head only for my enjoyment, then so be it. She is mine, and nothing in the world can take that from me until the day I die and then even so, I seriously fucking doubt it would leave me. It would have to escape through a pinhole, and even then, it would take days, weeks, because I have every piece of her in me, two bodies in one, and I would hide in the dark so karma couldn't find me, or insanity, or even morality, it would have to struggle and wrestle and slaughter every shadow that ever existed before I gave myself up to time, and I wouldn't let any friend or enemy know where I was.

This is what happens when I sleep. Every night.

Being alone drives me to the end of the world and I hate the destination.

I get up, go to the bathroom, splash water on my face. My hands are raw. My throat is so numb I can't even cough.

Why do I want someone who is no fucking good for me?

Why do I love her?

What has she done other than doing what she did, to us, to her, to our marriage? It's not just me. She has a part in this, too. The story goes both ways. Don't think that she was telling the right side of the story.

She is so beautiful she has made me done idiotic things, and it meant nothing because I did not - and could not - wind up with her. The thought of her with another lover, though, kills me. But what can I do? Would she like it, would she love it, would she hate it?

God, I wish I had never done any of this to begin with. I should have ignored her that night I met her. I could have let her go, like a bird in the wind, like a poem in a notebook that was meant for the trash, like war with no soldiers so it would go back to being peace.

I sit back on the toilet, I'm ready to throw up, I'm ready to do it again, I'm ready to lose.

part

three

*"Hi there."*

*"Oh. Hi there."*

*"That's a good book you're reading. I just got done reading it myself."*

*"Oh, yeah? Yeah, it's pretty good. I mean, Foer was always just one of those authors I knew I had to read and I'm finally getting around to it now."*

*"Safran."*

*"Pardon?"*

*"He prefers it if he's called Safran Foer. In regards to his last name. Not just the last."*

*"How do you know that?"*

*"I think I read it somewhere."*

*"Where?"*

*"I think in the newspaper. One of those spotlight articles?"*

*"Oh."*

*"Well, maybe not there. Maybe online."*

*"Huh."*

*"I'm not really sure. But I did read it somewhere."*

*"Oh. Well. Then I guess it must be true."*

*"Maybe it isn't true. I mean they could have made it up."*

*"That's also true. People benefit from lies."*

*"I guess so. I'm sorry, I'll let you go."*

*"No, it's ok..."*

*"No, I know what it's like to interrupt a reader. I really shouldn't do it. It's rude."*

*"Doesn't bother me any. It's nice to know people read these days."*

*"Yes, it is, isn't it?"*

*"It really is. People just rather do other things."*

*"It's a shame, yeah. Um, sorry, I'm really going to let you go this time."*

*"It really doesn't bother me."*

*"Yeah, but I'm working, so...I shouldn't be standing around..."*

*"Oh. Well, I guess I could see that."*

*"I hope you enjoy it."*

*"Yes, me too. It's good so far."*

*"It's different, that's for sure. Sorry again."*

*"You're alright."*

**Time passes.**

*"Is everything illuminated yet?"*

*"Pardon?*

*"Sorry, um, bad joke. I asked if everything was illuminated yet. The book. You're reading. I'm making a witticism. God, I'm sorry."*

*"No, no, heh, it's ok. Took me a while. I think my brain took a break. I'm not really comprehending reality right now. I'm stuck in this."*

*"Well, that means you're enjoying it."*

*"I guess so. I respond to books differently than other people."*

*"Like how? Like, with violence?"*

*"Oh, no, I guess I think too much. Interpretation. Literary theory ruined my enjoyment of literature."*

*"What's literary theory?"*

*"Oh, this happy horseshit where you apply these theories to books to help you understand the text and the author's meaning more. It's just an excuse to be intellectual."*

*"That doesn't sound fun."*

*"It's not. I can't even read Winnie the Pooh without a totalitarian bend anymore."*

*"..."*

*"That's my idea of a bad joke, heh. Sorry."*

*"College kid, are you?"*

*"Afraid so."*

*"Just up the road."*

*"Yeah."*

*"Skipping class?"*

*"You got me."*

"But you read even when you escape. You study even when you're away. You're a scholar down to your conditioned core."

"Aren't you a college kid?"

"I've lived here my whole life. Grew up in this town. See that college from my attic window all the time. Never had the money to go."

"I'm sorry."

"I'm not. I can learn plenty about life right here. Serving coffee. Getting stories from kids like you. Drunk or not, stoned or not, intellectuals or not. Never would have pegged you for one of those."

"You say it like it's a bad thing."

"Not trying to. Just my nature. Do you want your check?"

"No. I'm going to stay here for a little while more. If that's ok."

"Of course it isn't. I can't have you reading books in this diner. What would people say?"

"They would probably say, 'I want another cup of coffee but that waitress is talking to the idiot reading Foer'. Sorry, Safran Foer."

"They probably are. I'm sorry. I didn't mean to ramble."

"It's ok. I said it didn't bother me."

"It might, deep down. You're just too conditioned to tell me the truth, what with being college kid and all."

"That's a lie."

"There's you telling the truth again. You hide what you want to say, you talk like you actually like the Golden Rule. You're still a kid. You'll hide your feelings and lie your ass off. I bet you don't even like the book at all. You just went along with it because I said something about it. Am I right?"

"I don't know about all that, but I would like another cup of coffee. I'm still a paying customer. Since I don't have the check."

"Let me see what these people want first. After all, they're the ones who are ready to riot. They got things to do. They're too busy outside of this diner to be a smart guy intellectual."

**Time passes.**

"What, did you have to kill the coffee beans first?"

"Some would argue that I'm a pacifist. I don't have negative feelings about everything."

"That college thing, though. That kinda still stings."

"Oh, don't take it so personal. I didn't want to be offensive. I just am. I've had a lot go on in my life. I guess I'm jealous. I never went. You're lucky, I'm not."

*"What makes you think I'm lucky? How are you not lucky?"*

*"The reasons could fill a book."*

*"They could and they couldn't. Who would be the judge of that?"*

*"Judges, I guess."*

*"Not all judges can write long enough to judge properly. That's why they only talk. If they had to write down what they said all the time, it would lose meaning. They live in the moment."*

*"That doesn't make any sense at all."*

*"It does. One of my smart guy professors said that once. Think about it."*

*"I'm too busy pouring coffee and reading into people like you to think properly. I gave up thinking a long time ago. That's why I judge."*

*"Suit yourself. But stuff like that goes a long way."*

*"It doesn't matter in the long run."*

*"Existentialism, now, eh? One of the only theories that makes sense."*

*"What's that?"*

*"Think about it."*

*"Are you ready to go yet or what?"*

*"Well, I'm still waiting on that coffee."*

*"Next, you'll be asking for a piece of apple pie to go with it."*

*"You know, that does sound good. Since I'm skipping all the classes in the world, I got all the time possible. Heat it up, too."*

*"With vanilla ice cream."*

*"And a spoon. Keep that check."*

**Time passes.**

*"I just want to let you know I finished that novel. I am quite illuminated."*

*"Jesus. You're still here. Don't you have a beer bong to down, college kid?"*

*"No, I got a statue to push over and a panty run to go on, but since you gave me coffee, since you said hello, since you gave me a delicious slice of apple pie with vanilla ice cream, and a fork instead of a spoon, I feel like we reached that part of the conversation where we can tell each other our names. I'm *****."*

*"And what makes you think I want to tell you mine?"*

*"Because we've been sharing human feelings all day. We've been connecting on a whole bunch of shit all day. And when you go home tonight and you replay this episode in your head, you'll say to yourself, 'Shit. That boy I talked to all day today, when I was supposed to be*

*working, was really cute. He was worth getting fired over.'
And you'll sit by that attic window of yours and be bitter
about that college up the road and you'll say, 'Damn, how
I hate everything about the world' and you'll think about
how you want to change it and what better way to change
it? By leaving, right? But then you'll go into the real world
and you'll find that you can't judge people the way you've
been judging people here. All you see of that world is what
walks through that door. Drunk or not, stoned or not,
intellectuals or not, you see them come in droves and you
secretly wish that once, you could go up to that college
and share those views of yours with those people.
Because, you see, you are no different than them. In some
ways, you're smarter than half of those people I have class
with. Because you are fearless. You're illuminated. You
know what it's like to pick the human brain apart. You've
been coming over and flirting with me - no, wait, let me
finish, I don't care if you have tables, I'm on a roll. You've
been coming over here - slyly, you think - and you want to
see if I feel the same way about things like you do. It's a
test, it's a game. Isn't it? I'm sure you saw some of those
other people walk through this door and you say, 'Well, he
could be something.' He looks alright, but then as you talk
to them - over apple pie or whatever it is - you find out
that these people are shit. But I played along. I bit.*

*Because, yes, you're attractive. Because you're a great server. Because I think that you've met your match and you just don't want to admit it because there is not room enough in your bubble to include a person like me. Well, step out of that bubble. Join up with another bubble. See what it's like outside of this place. I'm not asking you to do anything crazy. I'm just asking you that if you've been fearless and illuminated up until this point, go the full mile. Fight. What was it for? Is it for saving yourself or is it saving an idea of yourself that you like to project? Go ahead."*

*"..."*

*"I overstepped a boundary apparently. I'm sorry. I probably came off sounding like a gigantic asshole. But I had to say it. This is what happens when I sit and think long enough. I come off sounding like this. Maybe that's the idea of myself that I project when I really want to be just myself. Forgive me. I'm going to go pay this and go back up to class."*

*"I'm ****."*

*"It's a pleasure to meet you."*

*"Likewise."*

*"I'm really sorry I said - "*

*"No, I'm glad you did. You, unfortunately, were one hundred percent correct. And I'm afraid to admit it*

sometimes, but yes, I'm jealous. Afraid. I've been hurt before."

"Who hasn't?"

"The point is that I just can't change at the drop of a hat. It takes time."

"So learn."

"It isn't that easy."

"Sure it is. Do you think I was born into being able to speak like that?"

"No, being an asshole takes plenty of time and lots of practice."

"Look, I said I was..."

"No, you listen. You are an asshole. You're right, and you're still an asshole. I came up to you to tell you that you were reading a good book and that I liked it, not to share and contribute to some disgusting chauvinistic fantasy where you think I'm flirting you all because you're horny and you can't get laid from some intellectual fucking walking boob job."

"Ok, I'm going to leave..."

"No, don't. I want to put you through the same embarrassment you just put me through. Jesus, what a show. I can't believe I went through with it as long as I did. How could you say those things about me? What gives you the right to think you're better than me, just *because you sit in some fancy classroom and learn about fancy retarded shit?"*

*"I never said I was better than you."*

*"In a way, you did."*

*"Well, I didn't."*

*"So what now? You're going to half-heartedly apologize and I'm going to half-heartedly accept it? And what now? Is this another episode in your fantasy life?"*

*"Regardless of what you think, I meant what I said. I don't put up fronts. This is how I am. And because you're so heavily invested in this argument right now means that you don't think I'm a total asshole at all. You're thinking that this is the most worthy opponent you've ever had."*

*"Shut the fuck up. You don't KNOW me."*

*"I'm telling you what I see. You're obviously bright. So don't get offended when you talk to someone first and they tell you what's on their mind. You started it."*

*"So we're playing that game. He started it, she started it."*

*"You want to keep making a scene? Because that's what we're doing. Everyone is staring."*

*"I don't care. They know me here. You're just an outsider. They'll never be able to understand you. They think you're just another puppet."*

*"And maybe I am. But I can speak for myself. And I'll show you my actions mean just as much as my words. It was a pleasure meeting you, \*\*\*\*. I'll show myself out. Don't take offense to what I said. But I meant it. That's what life is, isn't it?"*

**A week of time passes.**

*"Hey."*

*"Hi."*

*"Look, um, I know this is awkward. But I need to tell you some things."*

*"Ok."*

*"Can I sit down?"*

*"Aren't you working?"*

*"No, my shift just ended. I saw you came in, so I stayed."*

*"Ok, sit down."*

*"Thanks."*

*"So what is it that you have to say?"*

*"I know saying just sorry won't be enough."*

*"It could, if it's sincere."*

*"Look, drop that. Be honest with me, ok? Don't talk to me like a professor. I'm a human. There's a difference."*

*"I can agree with that."*

"Look, I made a scene. I won't apologize for that, because that's how I am. Certain things you just can't apologize for. It's your character, it's what makes you. Understand?"

"Yes, I can see that, as well."

"Ok. But I was harsh in my selection of words. That's choice. That I can apologize for."

"Fair enough. Apology accepted."

"I'm not finished yet. How do I want to word the rest of this?"

"Take your time."

"..."

"..."

"Ok, confession."

"Go."

"You were right. I was testing you. But don't think of me as a bitch."

"I don't. I barely know you."

"But you know me well enough to form an opinion of me as that 'bitch from the diner down the road.'"

"If you say so. But I haven't."

"Ok, whatever. The point is that yeah, ok, I may have come over to flirt with you, but not because you were just reading a good book. I never read the book."

"So what was it?"

*"I thought you were attractive."*

*"Thanks."*

*"Don't flatter yourself. You're not Jake."*

*"Who?"*

*"That guy in that Donnie rabbit movie. I can never remember his last name."*

*"Ok."*

*"But the point is, again, is that it wasn't because of just your looks. I saw something in you and I wanted to answer a question."*

*"Which is what?"*

*"It involves a game I play with myself. It' s an awful one. It's to see if I'm still beautiful or not. I can't believe I'm going to tell you this, but I was thinking about it all week, and if you came in here again, I swore to myself that I would tell you, and now, that that moment is here, you have to hear it all. Do you accept it?"*

*"Sure."*

*"It's a long story. I want to make sure it doesn't interfere with your literary whatever the hell it is."*

*"It's canceled for the week."*

*"Fine. Ok. The game involves me seeing if I'm beautiful. My mother was a beautiful woman. And the story goes is that my dad married her because of just her beauty. Her outer beauty, and at times, her inner beauty.*

*Because he saw only parts of her inner beauty, whenever she wanted to show it, and what he did see, he judged her wholeness based off of that. He could only judge what he saw. That's why all that nonsense you said about judging got me mad. It was because of personal experience. Anyway, the story goes is that he saw mostly her outer beauty. Her eyes, her body. All of that he wanted badly. He couldn't tell if it was lust or love, but he was attracted to it, and he was so concerned with the outer than he never cared about the inner, the intricate machine inside. Do you understand so far? Ok, so over the years. I saw that all unravel. All come apart. My dad loved beauty. But he did not love what made it work. Because he did not talk. He would rather do things that involved just the outer shell of people. He could take her to parties because she could turn heads. And she went along with it, because she knew she was beautiful and because she was smarter than him. The true power lay within her, but she could never tell him how she felt because he would not understand it. At all. It would be like talking to a brick wall. So my mother and my father had a kid. Who was born with the ability to do both of those things. To be beautiful and to be smart. And because she was both, she was too much for the both of them. That's why these two people, my parents, are divorced. That's why this beautiful girl lives alone and constantly has to ask herself, did she do something wrong? Is she really as beautiful as she thinks she is? But how will she find out if she doesn't open her mouth and talk? Does she just ask random men, or will they lie to her? How will she find one that will tell her the truth? And with most people, in most cases, they never look past the outer beauty. They can see me from the front, the cover, and want me. But they will not know me. Because they are stupid. Because they do not want to use effort, they do not want to move their limbs. They would rather stay within themselves and hope that I never leave that outer beauty, that I never go in myself and destroy them with what I truly have. So I read. I write. I do a million things I thought I would never do, in the wake of this shitty discovery about myself. It's why I never went to college. It's not just the money. I've been working here since I was 13. Long before I knew anything about myself like I do now. But the point is that if I went up there, and saw how ugly I was in the realm of all these beautiful people, even in the scope of their company, I would fall apart, because I'm not sure how beauty and intelligence can coincide without something hideous getting in the way. But you, from what I see, handle it so effortlessly. Fine, smile if you want, but you're a handsome guy. And you're smart. I'm jealous. I admit all that. But I talked to you because I wanted to see if you would think I was beautiful. Or that I was smart. I'm sure you've been through people before, but I wanted to see if I would be different. Whether or not you think I'm a total creeper now, or a bitch, you can certainly think that, I don't care. You don't have to come back here if you don't want to. I just had to tell you so I could be able to sleep at night."*

*"I don't think you're beautiful."*

*"..."*

*"I KNOW you're beautiful."*

*"Stop that."*

*"It's the truth."*

*"But I've heard that all before. Why is this one different?"*

*"Can I tell you a story that it's been told before?"*

*"What does that mean?"*

*"It's from a movie. It's not my original thought, but I don't care. It's going to say how I feel. Better than I ever could, I guess."*

*"Ok. Is it really weird?"*

*"Not as weird as Donnie Rabbit."*

*"That is a weird movie."*

*"Ok, so bear with me. There's a guy and a girl. And they're young. And in this movie, they're flirting off and on. They're trying to get on the same page, but they*

*stumble. And one afternoon, they meet in a bar. And she's been drinking. She's been saying some things that she discovers about herself. Her name sounds weird to her. She's afraid to see her therapist later because there's booze on her breath. And he catches up with her, he drinks too. They met because they had a writing class together. They couldn't stand each other at first, but it doesn't matter now, because they're connecting, and they share a moment in this bar, that maybe this could work, maybe that they can be together. They hastily shoot down the idea because of fear. She leaves to go to her appointment and she's walking down the sidewalk and he catches up to her and he's obviously trying to say how he feels because he's afraid. Because that's what life is. It isn't what I said it was earlier when I left last week. It's fear. We base our decisions off of FEAR. We just do. That's how it is. Anyway, he obviously wants to do something, and she tries to get it out of him. And he says to her, and I'm kinda paraphrasing, so bear with me, he says. 'The way I see it, if we were an old couple, that had been dating for years, I could lean over and kiss you on the cheek, and you would be delighted. But if I were to do that now, as a young couple, you would probably hit me.' And she looks at him really weird, and she says, 'What are you saying?' And he looks at her with a stone cold glare and he just simply says, 'I just wish we were an old couple so I could do that.' And she laughs. And he laughs. And she says, 'What?' like all nervous and stuff. And the movie ends. It fades out."*

*"I don't get it."*

*"Be with me, and you will."*

*"..."*

*"..."*

*"What are you saying?"*

*"I'm saying that because I know you're beautiful. I told you that story because beginnings mean a whole hell of a lot. It is so easy to create an ending out of something because it requires minimal effort. You can easily end a friendship based on a knee jerk reaction, a gut feeling, something emotional and quick. It can end and it doesn't hurt much to think about it. But beginnings are something else, something magical. They're wonderful. And I told you that because I think you appreciate the moral of that story."*

*"Which is what?"*

*"Which is take a chance. Be creative. Do something."*

*"You want me...to be with you?"*

*"I do."*

*"Why?"*

*"Because you told me that story and I know for a fact that you are genuine. You're a real person. Because what you think are real college-educated types up there, they are nothing like that at all. You think because they're smart that they're together. You think because they're beautiful that they're together. But that is far from the case, because they are conditioned. Just like me. They don't know what it's like to pour coffee and tell stories as great as yours. I don't mean great as in awesome. I meant great as in deep. There's pain in there. There's scars. And yours mean something because they are real. They were earned, do you know what I mean?"*

*"Don't make light of that. It's not funny."*

*"I'm not trying to say it is. I'm not trying to do that at all. But listen to me. I know what it's like to be around those people every day. And I don't like it. Did you see me bring a girl in here before? No. Because I know they don't like that story. The point is that being beautiful or smart has nothing to do with life. It's just excuses we tell ourselves to not care about what really matters."*

*"What matters?"*

*"This. Saying words. Talking back and forth. Because that's how you started this with me all along. It was never a question of beauty or intelligence at all. That's physical, mental. But how you started it, all of this,*

*came from your heart. That's emotional. People need to trust the emotional. And yes, you can argue that I'm one of those conditioned people. But I'm not so dead to the point where I can look at your story and just shrug it off. Some people do. And those are the people who see the outer beauty and don't care what's inside. But I do. I want to know more. I want to know more about the attic window, and how you came across that bullshit about him preferring be called Safran Foer. I want to know what makes you tick. And I thought about what you said to me before I left. I laid in bed and I became illuminated. I want to be able to show you what really matters. I want you to see that bitterness is not the answer to everything. And I was hoping you were still here. All I had was a name. But I want more."*

*"But I'm not the greatest person in the world. I don't know how to love."*

*"Does anybody? I know you've probably been through a lot. I have, too. But how can you put off the rest of your life based on fear?"*

*"But you said that's how people make decisions."*

*"Just because people do doesn't mean YOU have to. I don't have to, either."*

*"What's the basis of your decision-making?"*

"Opportunity. Chance. Luck. Anything other than fear."

"And how many women have you said all this to?"

"What does it matter? They're not here. All of this happens for a reason. Me sitting here talking to you. It's fate."

"Fate isn't real."

"So you're going to live your life off coincidence?"

"I didn't say that. Don't be an asshole."

"I apologize. But the point I'm trying to make is that you are different. I can see things in you. I think you'll be a happier person if you're away from here."

"This is my home. You don't live around me. You're just here to get what you need and get out of here and start your life. You only think you're right for me because you met me."

"What do you mean like that?"

"Ok, there's someone for everybody like that, right? Well, what if I'm in Vancouver and you live in Toronto? Across the country? We may never meet that other half, so wherever we live, we find someone that we want to be with, but not because of love. Out of fear of being alone. That's where the fear comes in, at least for me. We settle. That's all we do."

"Don't tell me you honestly believe in that."

*"I can believe in whatever I want to believe, don't act like that."*

*"But why settle? Why do you call it that?"*

*"Because that's how it is. How can a person's soul mate be in the same town, be within twenty miles of each other? How does that work? What if the person I love lives in another part of the world?"*

*"How will you know until you leave home and try?"*

*"Because who's to say that the other half feels the same way? What if they give up? What if they settle and wind up with someone they only half care about? Like my parents, of all people. And then I run into that person who supposedly is right for me and he says to me, 'well, I gave up, so spend the rest of your life being alone and in love with someone who doesn't love you back.'"*

*"How do you know that for sure?"*

*"Did you hear that story about my parents? Were you even listening? Or were you too busy worrying about what sounded right in your head?"*

*"Don't treat me like I'm some stuck-up fuck."*

*"But this is my whole point. I can't just give myself up like you can and go in search of the big love and constantly happy. The person of my dreams just isn't here. They just aren't."*

*"Then where are they?"*

*"I have no idea. They're just not here."*

*"..."*

*"..."*

*"So what now?"*

*"What do you mean?"*

*"All of what we told each other, that means nothing now?"*

*"I didn't say that. You asked what was on my mind. I'm telling you."*

*"But are you saying that because you believe in it, or because the fear is talking? What about your heart?"*

*"What about it?"*

*"What does it say?"*

*"It's saying I should have left here a long time ago. That I should have never said anything to you. I should have left you here with your stupid book and your stupid ideas and I should have just poured the fucking coffee and shut the fuck up."*

*"Now why do you have to put yourself down like that?"*

*"Oh, like you never self doubt yourself."*

*"Of course I do. I'm human. But I try not to."*

*"Why?"*

*"Well, what's the point of it?"*

*"You learn shit about yourself."*

*"There's other ways."*

*"Like how?"*

*"Open your mind and try to talk to someone who halfway understand what you mean and what you're going through."*

*"Oh, like who? You?"*

*"Yes, me. I told you everything I told you because I like you. If anything came out of that whole scene last week, it's that. I'll say it again, you are real to me. You're not fake. And whether or not you're too blind to see it, I do. And I'm getting loud because I care."*

*"So what am I supposed to do now? Just fall into your arms and accept everything you say because you told me a story and I told you a story and because of that connection, it all makes sense now, that you're my other half and that we're meant to be together and because of one fluke moment, we should fall in love?"*

*"I didn't say that. Just try it. What's so bad about that?"*

*"It's love. Humans are messy. We play games."*

*"Of course we do! But not everybody does that. I'm different. Do you like to think you're different?"*

*"All the time. I'm not like everybody else."*

*"Ok. So do it. Fall in love. Or develop feelings, however you do it. I admitted to you that I liked you. I'd like to take you out on a date."*

*"Oh, God."*

*"What?"*

*"Are you seriously fucking asking me out?"*

*"Yes, I am."*

*"Why?"*

*"Do I really have to tell you all that again?"*

*"What, that scene out of a movie? Give me a break."*

*"That scene says more about human life than anybody ever could. That story means a lot. To me, to lots of people."*

*"And that story about my parents - which is REAL and not a part of some fucking MOVIE - means more to me than anything else, so how can you put value on one over the other?"*

*"I never said they did. We combine them. We make them our own."*

*"You're talking like I'm dating you."*

*"Come on. Let's cut the bullshit. Right now. Let's get down to the straight story. If you don't give me a good enough reason why we shouldn't go on one date..."*

*"Because I don't think it'll work."*

*"Not good enough."*

*"What do you want me to say?"*

*"The truth. Give me your honesty, give me the part of you that makes you work."*

*"I don't do that. I can't give that. I don't know how to do any of what you're telling me. I've been hurt before."*

*"Be with me, and you'll be fixed."*

*"But how can you be so sure?"*

**A brief amount of time passes.**

*"If we were an old couple, you'd know."*

**Time pauses. She thinks. Time unpauses for the first kiss. Then, it passes.**

part

four

I should have known.

I could never fix the broken.

It would have never been forgotten. It would stay. Like blood. Back to blood, back to air, back to bones and roads we go. Back in oceans and papers and poems and things, back to where all of those things go. They were words but they remain. This is where my mind goes when I wake up. It isn't about daybreak, it's about heartache, heart break, a heart dripping blood into an endless place.

It's about all of these things, and if you don't think it is, then I believe you are sadly mistaken. When you fall in love with that person, you remember everything, and you think that nothing can hurt you. But you're wrong.

How you meet the love of your life is a moment you never forget. And that's mine. I took her out on that date the next day. And we ran away with the thrill of it all, lived off the energy and gasoline of the moment, took hold of the dream, rode it to the top, lived in the sweetness and the newness of it all. In a short amount of time, I had memorized her body and made sure that it fit to every whim I had created, whether it be superficial or not. I had gotten creative with myself, allowed myself to make up fantasies I had not previously allowed - I had given her a name that was synonymous to music. Sweeping, epic, grand orchestral music, but played at a very quiet level, just for me. It would stay in silent pockets for me to use when I was alone from her. It was beautiful, young love, and it would change of course over time, like things always do, but the wrinkles were too far away for me to worry about then. I was by and large more curious about the day to day operations with her - I wanted to know more about this machine, this collection of parts, that just so happened to bring me to my ultimate happiness. We were young. We thought we were everything, the opposite of what we swore not to become. Naturally, things took a different turn.

That restaurant conversation became a thing of glory for me at the time. I was so impressed with how I was able to correctly, accurately, so easily bring her to an understanding of love, when I myself, didn't even know what the hell it was I wanted. The funny yet sad thing was that it WAS a game. She played the game of her beauty, day in and day out. I would play a game where I dreamed about being a writer, but I only had ever written one thing – my wedding vows to my future wife. She - whoever she would have been then, there were a million possibilities - would have loved it and married me underneath the stars in a private ceremony for only a lucky few. My mind would race at the thought of making someone so happy and satisfied that I would have to do nothing else for the rest of my life except take the love I had and let it drown me a thousand times over.

I would never have to work or even breathe – I could just hold her hand and I would remember the image again and again. It was a drug, an addiction. I would have been so proud just to be able to whisper to a girl in a white dress that she was wearing just for me, and then, softly, after all the talking, I would kiss her gently on the lips, and we could fall back into a world that involved no city, no strangers, no knives, no dreams left scarred and broken at the hands of the insane. It would have been bliss. It would have been a philosophy with no strings attached. But we know with every beginning has an ending, and just like my game began, it ended so quickly, with the blunt pressure of realism. I would wake up every time I felt it, and I would look around and see nothing but empty faces of people who not once would ever think about reading anything I would write, whether it be above love or not.

But that's not the point, whether I can write it or not. It's about her. It's about when I met her, and I went back to my dorm room that night, slowly remembering the whole conversation, like the never-ending movie in my head, that I was unable to make myself write down even fake wedding vows or even imagine a fake wedding. I was bitten by something unshakable, glorious and groundless, something, well, beautiful. It was her. Some people say they do not believe in true love at first sight. Maybe it takes days, or weeks, or even a month or two. Some say that they have to live with the person for a while, or be with them until a certain time, to make sure that they are the right person. But for me, and her, I knew that night, counting the stars through the window with the fumes of whiskey on my lips, I could only imagine the things I would say to her next, if I were lucky to. And if she didn't appear in a certain amount of time, that I would find her, make an attempt to grab her by the shoulders, and tell her whatever bullshit I could have slung to her at the time. And that's where my downfall rears its ugly head, like other things. My double-sidedness, my inability to properly form a scenario where I am truly happy, fails, even when I am referring to the girl I wanted to spend the rest of my life with.

It's like when you meet someone, maybe you do quietly settle, against your heart's wishes. You say that it's only a stopgap, a brief lapse of time where you will allow yourself to just hold this person's hand instead of someone else, it's a brief encounter of two beings in a rain-soaked world and you just want shelter until the storm comes. But when the storm passes and safety comes, you stay with that person, because you are beyond just small settling, and you get comfortable with the idea that you have to stay with this person because you have defeated tragedy, and that is a memory. And the fear - which is what I was trying to stress to her that night - was that the fear of losing those memories, gaining new ones, and attempting the same thing with a new person is enough to scare people away from ever doing what they want to do. So maybe we were both right. We settle, we're afraid, we conflict, we don't really mean what we say, we fight until we pass out, and then the day begins anew but with the same problem burning inside. *We don't love each other, this just will not work out. It won't. Let's say it together. Wait. We can't, can't we? Ok, let's wait another day. Or lifetime.*

The reason that I look back at the time we met and see it with some disdain is that I should have been able to see that behavior she had - the argument the first time we met, the inability to understand what I was saying the second time we met - as humongous warning signs. She was mocking me. She was standoffish. She was selfish and perhaps a little bitchy. But then again, people have their flaws. I should have worked around them better or just accepted them. But love - the old bullet - had snuck it again. It blinded me. So I learned to love those things that

I just hated about her. And I thought, with time, they would get better. And I should have been able to beat my head against the wall with the thought until I fell - that never, ever happens. When does it ever work out like that? The savior, the hero, the princess, the fairytale. All of the plot elements, intricate, like building blocks, we are taught them early and they are reinforced - love conquers all. Bullshit.

I'm sorry. I don't want you to see this like it's a sin. Or that beautiful things become scandalized and unusable over time. I don't want to disrupt sacred beliefs you hold high. I don't want to ever suggest that love - yours and the ones you have - dematerializes in front of your face. You will succeed because you are not me. You are stronger people with more solid convictions, who believe in the power of staying together, who want to fight for the concepts that you were raised with. Family. Marriage. Loyalty. I, for one, have lost all of that, or one would argue, for those who are unfortunate enough to know me, that I never had it. I had raised myself. I fought through caves just to get to moss. But I'm fucked in the head to the point where I am bitter towards complete strangers, and they see it, and they go farther distances than they had intended just to get away from me, and I never want that to happen, but it does, and I have to learn to carry the burden and cope with the strain, instead of it. I don't want to fix what's wrong with me. I just want to learn to cope with it better. There is no sense in choosing death as a coping ability. So I sit quietly. I write long stories in hopes they will help and heal people in my position. There is nothing wrong with living with a fucked up heart. But there is something wrong with wanting to ruin the good hearts for those people who have them, and that's not what I'm trying to do. I'm just farther back in the trenches than you. I'm ready to see the end of the world alone, if I should live to see that point in the timeline of our humanity. Just remember this when you go to a rough patch. You will never, ever, ever, have it as bad as me.

I have nothing but nothing, anything, and everything to give you.

I get out of bed finally and I move to the window. The city has stayed the same, despite slowly dying. It will continue its industrialized slouch to metallic, underfunded graves. I will never know how I made it out here. I was always a country person. She was, too. That's how we met, for God's sakes. The irony is enough to kill the sky. And this is where I go when I have to run, to show the world that I can run, and my running has proven successful, because her search has not led me here. It'll stay this way, for a very long time. I go into the bathroom to try to make myself look halfway like a human being, because today, I do not. I look slowly into the mirror, and I count the bags under my eyes, the yellowness to my face and teeth, I see the lines in my face and I am able to trace them perfectly.

Yesterday's events get to me and I begin to cry to my own self.

I know why I want the past, to remember and retell it so much. It's because the past is the past, it's already happened. It's familiar, I know what happens, she says this, I say that, I know what the ending will be. The future, it's unstable, it's scary, we have no idea what happens next, it can become anything, that's why we don't want it. But the past? It's a beautiful fucking thing. I sense myself retreating back into that world for a little while, and I don't think I'll mind it. Despite it being full of pain. That, I'm sure, is why it's so special. It heals and hurts, it does nothing to you, it cancels itself out. I love the past. I think I always will. But the future? I think that's going to wind up being something that just isn't easy.

I knew this would happen. I'm a broken record. It's a wonder I made it this far, on my own, without anyone's help. Well, hers, for a while. But even she couldn't save the disaster, much less make sense of it. Maybe she was the smarter one. Maybe she made herself as bad a person as she could just to get me to be worse so I would leave. Good God. Maybe I should give her more credit.

Maybe I should stop dragging her name through the mud.

Because yesterday, she could have done worse than what she did. She could have killed me. She could have never shown up and she could have left me live in wonder, make me think she died in an accident or she was in bed with another man. She could have lied. She could have slit her wrists in front of me, staged murder, lived long enough to tell me the name of another man she was with, or long enough to say that she loves me, only for me to feel mercy and wish for forgiveness, and before she would accept, she would die. And I look at these scenarios and I actually think them. Imagine them, play them out, direct them for people. Why would I? Why would I wish that kind of life for someone as beautiful as her? I wasn't lying when I said she was beautiful. That may be the only thing I ever meant that I said to her. That and "I love you". For some time.

I think of her pouring coffee for me and I feel so much regret.

But then I think of her denouncing things I worship, and I grit my teeth.

Then I think of her, getting ready for a date, brushing her hair, getting ready, getting clean, and I melt with desire.

Then I think of letting the darkness grab her, and I give myself grief.

I was so, so fucking close to feeling those lips again and going back to a college diner to discuss books, music, lay in my dorm room waiting for her to knock so I could run out of bed to greet her, seeing her choice of clothes, walking through campus, and watching the conditioned people walk past to their mechanic lives, discussing marriage, running through the rain to see surprises not meant for people like us, discussing life without evil, impure thoughts such as my own, and discussing her eagerness to fall in love with a man willing to protect her, and not one that would wind up like her father, one that would love her because he would mean it.

I think of that last bit and the tears fall faster. The sink begins to fill. My heart begins to empty more, which I didn't think was possible.

What a way to live the only life you're given.

But it's my choice. So don't feel sorry.

I walk back into the bedroom and look at my cell phone. No messages. I expected as much. She was still sleeping off the alcohol. Dreaming, I'm sure, of nightmares and fond memories of us in that apartment. Maybe the kiss was living large in her head just as much as mine. Come along, my shadow must be saying to her. I never left in the same place. And when she goes to open up, here comes the static. And her pain is not eased. She is left standing, shuddering at the thought of going back to the room alone. And when she does, she sees my name, written a million times, attacking her until oblivion.

Again, those scenarios. I have to stop.

In order to clear my mind, I start getting ready for the day. I guess it's painfully obvious at this point that I have no job anymore. I had to quit it when I left her, so she wouldn't come and find me, show up in an effort to fix things. I found the cheapest apartment I could find in the city and I'm living off my parents' inheritance they left me when they passed. I made an attempt to start a writing career - why, I have no idea. This has been the only thing I could even start. I guess it's because of the terrible source of inspiration. It doesn't matter, I guess, in the long run, because my new job turned out to be hiding, concealment. I could not let her find me. I had to do everything I could to cover my tracks, stop a paper trail, made sure my closest friends did not tell her when she would ask. I know that's psychopathic behavior. But if you're going to disappear, you have to cover all the bases, no matter how hurtful. You have to make sure that you stay gone. I know you don't like hearing it, but it's just a fact of life. You know that feeling that when you break up with someone, and you swear on your life that it's ok if you see them again shortly thereafter, somewhere public so it isn't personal, and then when you see them, no matter how they look, whatever they're wearing, the feeling floods you, and it gut punches you, and all you want to do is slink in the floor. Your tongue becomes sandpaper, cotton, numbness. You sweat uncontrollably. You cannot move. And they're staring at you. And you're all shaken up and they're ok. I didn't want that. And neither did she. So I took to hiding. And it has become remorseful and painful, yes, but not as much as going through that.

So what do I do now? I sit inside all day and I write. Like I said, most of it has been this, and it's my first time, so you'll have to go along with it. I never promised I would be a literary master or some award-winning author. I just want to be a realist, to last long enough to be respected, or remembered, whichever comes first or last. Even if you never read this, or ever see it, maybe you'll hear about it from someone, the myth, the urban legend that there's a bundle of paper floating around there in the city that contains some answers and questions about love, how to fix them, how to embrace it, how to win the girl of your dreams back, how to edit the pain well enough to take it in small doses throughout your life instead of all at once. Has anybody heard anything about that, strangers will ask strangers, but nobody will know, because nobody will care, because not everyone is as screwed up as those people who willingly quit their jobs and their wives just to write words down on paper. No one is that messed up, they'll say. Who would do that? People like that don't exist.

But they do. They really do.

That was another source of contention in the beginning for her and I. After we started dating, that day I kissed her in the restaurant in front of everyone - which, fine, I will admit, was the pinnacle of my love life up to that point - we had run into the problem of me not being able to see her every day. Even though we lived practically in the same college town, her just down the road and me in the dorm, I just couldn't make the time to do it. I was in my senior year at that point, so I was in six classes a semester, all of them for my major, all of them the toughest courses I ever had, writing papers every week, studying, sapping my time up, and she would want to come down to her place and do whatever. Now, I know it sounds like a juvenile problem, one that would easily be fixable if proper communication was involved, but we just hadn't gotten to that point where we would be comfortable in saying what was needed, so we either sidetracked around the issue or just agreed that the important things would wait, like my classes. She would convince me to drop whatever I was doing to come down and see her at work, or she would find me in the library, push all my books to the floor, and smother me with her love. Which I didn't mind, but when I was in the middle of a certain assignment, it would be a little bothersome. Which, she sulked about, and then she would walk away, and I would spend another night alone, dreaming instead of doing. But then the next day would come, and everything would be fine, until the same problem came up. Now, I know what you're thinking. If we had acted like adults instead of kids, do the responsible thing and properly talk about it, maybe I would have been able to have a better marriage. But, I didn't do any of that. I was more interested in the feelings I was getting now, instead of in the future, because honestly, she didn't see anything worthwhile about futures.

Just like that daydream I had about us in the woods I fantasized about earlier. She never wanted to have any talk about the years ahead. It was always *now, now, now*. Any sort of talk about it and she would shrink up, crawl into a shell, and wait until I forgot about it. Which I never did, because it was the only thing I wanted to clear up. Well, love is ok for a while, but after some time, you have to get into the big things, because, well, you have to make plans, even though sometimes that's a joke, too. *How do you make God laugh? You make a plan.* We all hear it a thousand times, but it's insanely true. Still, that's basing a decision off of fear, instead of practically, so we're back to square one. I would still want to come up with a solution anyway - *where do we go after I graduate? Do I stay here with you? Do you move back home with me? Where are the jobs going to be?* - and every time, she would pull the blankets back over her head, pretend to sleep, and I would get out of bed to write or read a book.

Writing was another taboo subject. She would always be over my shoulder, reading, trying to see what I was writing about. Was I ever writing about her, did she want to know. Is that a new poem or a new story about me or us? Half the time it was no, and whenever it was, she would never let me hear the end of it. Until, finally, one day, we had it out:

*I was sitting in the library late one night. I had just gone to the pay phone in the lobby and called her down at the diner to tell her that I wouldn't be able to come over until late tonight; I was working on a thesis paper for a literature class. She was disappointed, but she took the news quickly since it was busy. As I hung up the phone, I winced at the lie, since it was easy and she wouldn't be unable to distinguish if it was true or false, but I calmed myself down with the thought that sometimes these things happen, and not to look into it too much. She'll understand one day when you became a famous writer. So I smiled, went and got a cup of coffee from the student union, and sat down at a table to begin work.*

*About an hour into it, as the library started to clear out and only the serious scholars stayed, I had just drank the final gulp of sugar and cold coffee and choked on it when a pair of hands came crashing down on my shoulders and neck.*

*"Guess who!" I heard her playfully shout. There wasn't a lot of people around so I guess it was ok, but still, it's a library - those childhood six inch voices are still sacred to some.*

*I spun around and saw her goofy, wide smile. She had just left work, it seems, a dirty apron still around her waist, her hair messy, her makeup a little off, but still energetic, still happy. I could see a burn mark on her left arm from a hot plate she must have mishandled. I could see that she was wanting to play around, and while normally I would have welcomed it, I just wasn't in the mood. I admit, I was caught off guard. But it was too late now.*

*"Shh!" I said, "this is a library."*

*"Guess who!" She whisper-shouted.*

*"I give up."*

*"It's me!"*

*"That's right. It is you! How are you?"*

*"I thought you said you were busy."*

*"I am, very much so."*

*"A busy beaver."*

*"So busy I could be sick."*

*"So busy you could be dead."*

*"So busy I don't know whether to shit or piss."*

*"You're not working on your paper."*

*"That's because I'm whisper-shouting with you."*

*"No, no. Before that. You're only sitting here with a pen and a notebook. You have no books here. You lied, mister. You lied, you lied."*

*"Pants on fire."*

*"Burning."*

*"Blazing."*

*"Call the fire department."*

*"Call the whole force."*

*"That's right. And I'll make sure those pants are off later." She sat down next to me at the table and tried to see what I was working on. I instinctively pulled it away, a move I had down pat thanks to many instances of practice.*

*Normally, she wouldn't get so offended - she'd play it off like it didn't bother her - but I guess my attitude really put her off tonight.*

*"What is your problem?" She asked harshly.*

*"I don't have a problem," I spat back.*

*"There you go. You're snapping at me. Aren't you happy to see me?"*

*"I'm not snapping at you."*

*"Yes, you are, you always do," she said, pushing her hair back with her hand. I could see the burn mark better. I took her arm gingerly and she frowned, but when I kissed it, she smiled a little more, but I could tell that I was not going to get out of it that easily. "Aren't you happy to see me?" She said again.*

*"Of course I am," I said, and I went to give her a peck on the cheek next.*

*She turned away and I could tell she was holding back tears. Sensing an argument, I packed up my stuff and I took her by the hand and led her into a quiet study room around the corner. There, she could yell if she wanted to. Although, I was hoping to avoid it at any and all costs. But, this was a point in the relationship where something had to be nipped in the bud, and it might as well be now.*

"Why do you get so mad about that?" I said to her as she sat down with her back against the wall, choking back her sobs. "I'm not doing anything to hurt you."

"Yes, you are. You won't share a single thing with me. I want to know what you do. I care. I want to be a part of it."

"I understand that. I really do. But there are just some things that I don't want to share."

"Why? Are they about me?"

"No, and stop that. Quit being paranoid."

"Don't tell your girlfriend to be paranoid. It doesn't help her."

"Ok, well, then stop being anxious and nervous and worrisome."

"That doesn't help me either."

"Well, God, what do you want me to say? I'm not trying to hurt you. Look, I'm not going to fight anymore about this. I know this makes you upset, but this is just something about me that has to be a secret."

"Well, why? It's just words."

Mistake number one on her part. "Um, no, it's not just words. My writing is just something that's a part of who I am. And I like to keep it safe. I know that you want to see it, and I obviously trust you, but I can't give it up so *easily. It's like some things you hold close to you that you don't want me to see."*

*"I share everything with you. I don't hold anything back. I don't hide a fucking thing. I want you to see my life."*

*"And I'm very grateful for it, trust me. I love it. But I just can't do the same."*

*"Then what's the fucking point of being with you then?"*

*Mistake number two. "Excuse me, what did you just say?"*

*"Oh, you heard me," she said, standing up now, still leaning against the wall. She held her burned arm as if I was the one that gave it to her. Her face was red, bright red, almost like it was about to bust through with blood. She was starting to transform into a fighter. I had gotten close to this point, but never made it yet. Now I was to see, now I was to experience. I threw my stuff down on the floor and leaned against the other wall, taking position. Here we go. The thing about war, you remember it so vividly, you don't let it leave you, but peace, that goes by like a blink, and you struggle like hell to hold the fabric of it after it passes.*

*"No, I don't think I did. What exactly did you say to me? And use the same small words. So I know you understand them, too."*

*"God, you're such an asshole," she muttered with wrath. "I said. What's the fucking point of being with you? Which, now, that I'm seeing you now in your real state, it's a question that has much validity to it. There, did you like that word, Mr. Fucking Important?"*

*"Alright, you watch yourself. I didn't want it to get this far. I really didn't. But that little comment just pushed it to that point. Do you really want to see how mad I get?"*

*"Why, what are you going to do? I know you would never hit me."*

*"You're right. But I would think an awful lot about it."*

*"So what is the fucking point of being with you? Huh? I mean, every time I try to get you to open up, you just won't do it. It's like your stoic, you're a robot, you're a part of some secret conspiracy with yourself and only yourself. Why do you do this? You have no problem writing down your feelings, why can't you tell your girlfriend? Why does she have to do things like this to get you to be able to talk?"*

*"I'm talking right now."*

*"You know what I mean. Every night I know you lay there, wide awake in bed, and I'm sleeping, and I try to get you to hold me, and you always come up with some bullshit reason why you just won't do it. I try to get you to tell me about your childhood and you won't do it. I try to get you to tell me about the important things in your life and you just won't ever say a goddamn word. I barely know anything about you. You came into my life completely unannounced - which, by the way, I'm starting to goddamn regret - and you're a completely wonderful boy who makes me feel beautiful and I want to embrace that and be able to show people I know that you're this great person, but how can I do that if you won't open up and just say what's on your mind? Why do you have to run? Why do you have to hide when something great comes your way?"*

*"Are you finished yet?"*

*"No, as a matter of fact, I'm fucking not," she said, slamming the table. Thank God no one could hear us in that room. It was starting to get heated. I knew this would go on past the night. This would carry over for days. I knew I had done something wrong even though I knew I didn't, and that right there, was the catalyst for the first rift in our relationship. You know those times when you're with your lover. You know you're in the clear, you think*

*you have good intentions in doing something, like doing something secret behind their back but for all the right reasons, and then it just all blows up in your face. Trust me, there is never such thing as good intentions. It bites back, you become the prey, despite your heart doing what it's meant to do - care.*

*"Well, then, continue. I'm enjoying this."*

*"Don't be like that."*

*"Be like a child. Don't drag me down to your level."*

*"What level?"*

*"Aren't you even aware how immature you're sounding? Some fucking college boy. I should have known."*

*"Well, I guess that's the final point of your argument. Because we've evolved into name-calling and I told you so and all of that bullshit. First off..."*

*"Should I sit for this?"*

*"Do whatever you want."*

*"Ok, I just want to make sure, because you're actually going to say something to me for a change, and I want to prepare myself - "*

*"Don't get cute."*

*" - for the big fucking speech."*

*"Oh, like the one I gave you that first day we met? If I recall..."*

*"Yeah, just like that one, because that's when I knew you had a tongue -"*

*"...you really didn't care much for that one..."*

*" - and you knew how to use it for something other than between my legs."*

*"And you don't seem to complain about that, do you?" I admit, I was not choosing my words carefully. You can think of me however you want now. It's all in the wind at this point. I'm a disgusting human being. And I made fun of her this entire time and I call her the hypocrite when I am. So I guess I shouldn't paraphrase from here on out. I'll recreate a little better. Give this all a new sound for you. See what you think of it.*

*"Because that's what we're talking about, you know," she said sarcastically.*

*"My big speech, as you so call it, that I gave you that day, was to wake you up."*

*"You might want to choose your words a little better," she said, eerily echoing my thought at the time. Proof that we were meant to be together, or just coincidence, you decide. I call it all a happy accident.*

*"Why?"*

*"Treat me like a girlfriend. You don't have to talk to me like you're talking to one of your drunken dorm room fucking friends."*

*"Oh, so you mean more condescending?"*

*She sighed a really deep sigh. She took in a lot of breath before she said her next bit. I didn't realize it, but I was starting to lose the argument. She had been sitting, but her hands were folded, her legs crossed, like a student. I was standing, hands on the back of a chair, shaking uncontrollably. It might have been the temper. It might have been the disappearing momentum. It might have been realizing that I love this girl and I should not talk to her like I had been doing. Whatever it was, I had to admit, she was right, and if I was going to win this fight, I would have to find a different scheme. But then, that right there - "winning a fight" - that shouldn't even enter into a healthy relationship's language. There is no such thing. Compromising, maybe. But not outright winning. That's just superiority, Neanderthal mentality. There's no place for it anywhere.*

*"I'm doing everything in my power right now not to hurt you. And you know damn well what I'm talking about. Women. They can do a lot of dangerous things and I believe you are well versed enough to know that we are the fairer sex, but absolutely and by far the most*

*dominant. And I know you're going down a road, by your own volition, that could spell out horrible results for you. You're not fully aware of it because your temper both blinds you and leads you. But I'm here to tell you that I see the full path in front of you, and you're in for a world of pain if you keep going this way, if you keep saying these things. You're trying your best to hurt me right now, and I don't know why, but I am going to tell you a few things should you choose to continue this way." Her voice dropped down to a whisper. I know why - in order to make me listen, slowly, intently, carefully. "For reasons that I can't explain right now, I love you. That is the first time I am able to admit it in words, even though we have been dating for such a short amount of time. I've thought about it, I feel it, I know it in my heart, and my heart does not lie to me because I am able to tell truth to it enough for it to recognize no such thing as a lie. It might also be the last time I say that I love you, because depending on where you go and how you handle that confession, I might walk straight the fuck out and leave you here with all of this. All of whatever it is you hold dear in that" - she pointed at my chest - "heart of yours. Whatever you call it. I've let you get away with quite a bit right now. I will admit that. And maybe I am being a little selfish, a little bitchy, a little clingy. Whatever. I will learn. You apparently are going down a different thought process. But I am going to let this be known to you. And it is the only time I am going to say it. Women are able to hurt men. So deep, so painfully well that the scars will last well into your best years as a ghost. And women are also able to love men, very well, very beautifully, to where their souls - or whatever you believe in - are able to outlast eternity, holding hands, doing whatever it is they do. The fantasy is yours. I'm getting to the point. Don't sneak a glance at your watch. This is my time now. I don't want to hurt you. Because I love you. See? See how easy that was the second time around? This is what happens when you talk, when you say these things out loud, these things called your feelings? It becomes much easier, and you come to accept them a little easier, and then it's all ok. For everybody involved. So people don't have to scream and argue with each other all the time. But hurting you? That comes much easier. And I think you know how I can hurt you. I can make you think about me even when you want to forget. I have entered into your mind so well as a central character that if you were to graduate and never see me again, you would still wake up thinking of me, wishing I was next to you. And that's not an egomaniacal thing to say. That's just the truth. Women have that effect. The minute you admitted I was beautiful, the minute I entered into your sexual fantasies, the minute that you and I ever talked, I became a part of you, and you yearn, and your heart breaks and races at every pause, waiting for me to speak, because you use that voice to help you when I'm not around. Women haunt men. They become their everything. Even if we never get past this point, you will still think of when you could have turned this all around to save me. Am I right? So think very carefully. Because I do love you. And you said you wanted to be an old couple, and if I were to be with you, you'd fix me. Well, I don't know how that's working out for you, but for me, I am now telling you that I'm going to fix you. For better or worse, it's your choice. I'm making it very easy for you. Remember that word? Easy. Etch it into your story. Make it your own, if you want. But remember. You're standing in front of me. So how do you want to continue? What's your next step?"*

*I was able to remember that so well because of her elegance. She spoke no louder than a normal conversation between two people having lunch, or someone talking to a relative in the hospital. It had such lucid finality to it that I thought maybe it was a thesis or a paper or the final words of someone else spoken. It did not sound like her, but at the same time, I knew it was, and I think that power was enough to floor me. It did make my heart break and race at every pause. I was stuck to the* point where I didn't know if I had died. I was listening so hard that my knuckles turned white, my mouth went dry. My shaking stopped. But I couldn't even imagine a world now without not having heard that speech. I didn't know if she was the best person ever or the worst person ever. Angel, devil, bitch, goddess - she could have been any of those things, I would have taken either one and made a strong case for it. But all I know is that I had been simply out called, out done. What could I do to best that? What would any man do? What would any person do? I had simply underestimated her. I had been wrong - she did not meet her match that day in the diner, but I had met mine. And I knew right there that change was necessary in order for me to love myself, and to love her. I did the only thing I knew how to do.

I started to move towards her. I couldn't make it, my legs buckled. I sat down in the nearest chair, still a chair between us, like we were deliberating, negotiating a contract. I was speechless. I cupped my hands together and I was humiliated, but I pressed forward.

"I love you, too," I said for the first time, to her face.

She nodded slowly.

"And I believe it takes a big man to admit that he is wrong."

*"It does," she said with a sultry bent.*

*"And I will admit I was wrong about certain things."*

*She cocked her head and gave a little frown-smirk combination.*

*"I wasn't speaking to you very nicely."*

*"No, you were not."*

*"And respect is a big issue."*

*"It is an extremely big issue."*

*"So I was remiss in the fact that I did not respect you enough to talk to you like a human being - "*

*"A girlfriend, I believe, is what I said."*

*"Fine. A girlfriend. And I should have been able to trust you enough and be comfortable enough to speak like an adult instead of a drunken...whatever it is you said."*

*"Yeah, I forget too," she said, more smirking than frowning.*

*"So I am sorry. Please forgive me. I was out of control. I had let my anger get the best of me. That is never a pretty thing, you know."*

*"It happens to the best of us, dear," she said, and she reached for my hand.*

*I pulled back, and she immediately was concerned, like I had struck her. I wasn't going to let her have complete control. That would have said something horrible about me.*

*"I'm not quite finished," I said quietly. I didn't realize that I had been pushing back tears this entire time. I wiped them away with a hand and I went back to cupping them, just because I didn't want her to have them quite yet. She slunk back in her chair, began to shield herself with whatever armor she had left in her body.*

*"I'm to believe that we just had a major breakthrough in our relationship right now," I said. "Do you feel the same way?"*

*She nodded, then: "Yes, I do."*

*"Sometimes these things have to happen, as much as we don't like them to, they do."*

*"That's right."*

*"I don't like seeing you upset."*

*"I don't either," she said, and a few tears started to come for her, too.*

*"So we have to start fixing each other, yes?"*

*"Yes we do."*

*"And this is a start."*

*"Absolutely."*

*"So here's what I am going to say to you, since you want me to talk."*

*"Only if you mean it."*

*"I do," I said, and I gave her my one hand, and she smiled sadly. Tears fell onto both of our hands as she was preparing herself for my oncoming words.*

*"I know that you may not see it like this, but you have been the best girl I have ever had, in my life, out of anyone else, out of anyone I could ever dream of."*

*"But how?"*

*"You just are. You're striking a huge hole in my heart right now. You're staking a claim. You're writing your name on it. You just are. I can't get into how. But I guess the easiest way to say is that yes, you've begun to haunt me."*

*A little giggle escaped from her lips.*

*"And I know you may want to hear the romantic side of me, the side of me that gets deep into this shit where I say all these wonderful things, and I'm not saying you won't ever hear it, because some day, I guarantee, you will. You will." I squeezed her hand harder to illustrate my point. Show her that I care. "But I'm just not that kind of person to say it all the time."*

*"But why?"*

*"I don't know. I always was. I can't describe it."*

*"Ok. Go on."*

*"And I want to see this relationship to continue. There is potential."*

*"Yes, there is."*

*"I'm glad you see it that way. I really do."*

*"But, I do believe there has to be changes."*

*"What kind of changes?" She said.*

*"Things that you and I are going to have to accept about us."*

*"Like what?"*

*"You want me to talk more. I understand that. And I would like to learn how to, in time. But for now, all I can say is that it's one of the things that I am working on, and well, it's going to take a bit of time. Patience. It is a virtue, and it's a friend. We can't just throw it aside, yes?"*

*She nodded. The tears were slowing. We were approaching happiness, acceptance. What a foreign concept. I had to keep going in order to keep this alive.*

*"You also want me to talk about my writing," I said finally.*

*She nodded. "I know that I was overstepping..."*

*"Shhh, it's ok."*

*"It's not ok. Don't say it's ok. I was out of line."*

*"No, you weren't," I said, "I probably would have done the same thing were I in your position. It's natural, people to be curious. And God, it should have been a question I could answer easily for you. But I made it*

*difficult, and that I'm afraid, is something that will never change. I can't change that."*

*"Why not?" She looked at me, confused.*

*"You can't ever ask me what I write about. For your sanity and mine."*

*"What are you talking about? I don't get it. Help me understand it."*

*"Look at what happened to you when you found out that I wasn't going to show you what I was writing about. You lost it. I never saw you get so mad before. It was unreal. And I don't want to see you like that. And I don't think you like how you got either. Am I right?"*

*She nodded.*

*"It's like...it's like if I were to walk into your house, and you would show me all the things that mean everything to you, and if you sat there and told me the whole history of everything that you held sacred, and I just shrugged it all off, what would you do?"*

*"Get mad, probably."*

*"Because why?"*

*"Because you wouldn't believe me. Because you make fun of it. Because..."*

*"Because it's something that means something only to you. And giving it to someone so quickly without thought lessens the value of it."*

"But that's not true at all, some people hand down things to others, and people give each other things all the time."

"Ok, maybe I didn't word it right. But this is my point. That story about your mother and your father, the one you told me at the diner?"

She nodded.

"I know that is probably one of the more important things in your life."

"It is."

"And I don't want to touch it. It's yours."

"But I shared it with you. It's a part of you now."

"Yes, I agree with that. But the thing is that you can easily share things with people. But do you think if I shared something insignificant with you, like a toothpick or something, would you want to have it any longer than you had to?"

"You really, really need to work on your metaphors."

I had to laugh. "Ok, yeah, I am, but ok. See. Sharing something and letting someone have something are two different things. It boils down to experience. If I share a meal with you, it's experience. If I let you read a story I wrote, or have a story I write...it might not mean *the same to you as it does to me because it didn't come from you."*

*"But it came from you, and I love you."*

*"But you love it automatically, and that's not the point of things."*

*"Why not? Isn't love about sharing everything completely?"*

*"Not all the time."*

*"That is a bitter thing to say," she said.*

*"Maybe it is. But I don't see it that way. You can share things like food and clothes and maybe even some ideals. But you have your own set of morals as I do mine. What if some day down the road we get into something that we cannot fix together?"*

*"You lost me."*

*"What if I die?"*

*"Don't talk like that. It's absurd."*

*"It's reality. What if you die?"*

*"Stop that," she said, dropping her head, probably holding back a tear. Obviously I meant a lot to her. She spent most of her time dreaming about me, I'm sure. While I'm in class, fighting literary fires, she's working at the diner, burning her arm, thinking about when I can kiss her again. When we sleep on horribly cold nights, she pulls the blankets tighter, think they're my arms, and I'm in my*

*room, stuck on work, thinking about how she could make me the happiest man in the world if only I could let her. Maybe she saw us living out in the country, doing ordinary things, which would make me happy, but it doesn't fix everything. It just makes us run from what matters. Which, I know now, the irony is enough to drown the world. But it's her dream so I can't mock it. I'm sure she saw us doing incredible things, entering places together, and showing them all that we've done it, despite the fact that no one around will know who we are. I know that I had done something well enough to make her want me, and that's half the battle sometimes. She loved me. That's all that I had to know. Knowing more than that would not help matters.*

*"I'm not trying to upset you," I said, as I lifted her head back up with a finger, looking her in the eye. "I just want us to see reality."*

*"Maybe I don't want reality."*

*"You have to. It's all around us."*

*"I don't want us to die. We're so young."*

*"Ok, fine, but what if I like disappear?"*

*"Disappear?"*

*"What if I go missing?"*

*She snorted. "How could you go missing?"*

*"It's a possibility. What if I get lost somewhere and you have no idea where I went? That's what we can't fix together. We have to both be strong and independent on our own so we're able to do these things. That's why we can't share everything. Because then we become dependent on each other and whenever the one goes...the whole institution falls to pieces."*

*"Do you really think like this?" She asked me quietly, somewhat in shock.*

*I could only nod. "All the time."*

*"I don't think that's very healthy."*

*"It is what it is. I'm not proud of it, but then again, realists never are."*

*"So what does this all have to do with your writing, your secrets, and my secrets? How is this all connected?"*

*"You just have to trust me."*

*"I do."*

*I waved her off.*

*"Don't do that, it's fucking rude," she said, her anger coming back.*

*"How do you trust me?" I said to her. "With what I do to you? Push you away sometimes? Don't say things half the time? And how do you still trust me?"*

*"I do because..."*

*"You love me."*

*"I do, yes," she said, exasperated. "Look, I feel like we're talking in circles here. And I don't want to do that. Not now, not ever. I don't like doing it. So let's just get to the point. I don't want to be here anymore and I don't want to fight with you. I guess what you're saying is that there are some things that won't ever change, we just have to learn to cope with them and that's just how it is."*

*"In a blunt way of saying it, yes. We just have to cope."*

*"I don't know if that's for the best, but I'm going to go along with it."*

*"I love you," I said to her, in a weird plea to keep this going just a bit longer. I wanted her to really understand that I was not trying to be a selfish prick, but that I wanted her to see the disgusting reality of it all, and that whole life cannot be build off fantasy dreams and romantic wishes, that sometimes, in love, we hurt each other because we do not know what we want half the time. It's stupid, yes, and moods change every day, but we just have to adapt. If we were to change ourselves daily, in a month we would forget who we were. I started to say that to her, but I backed off. All I said was: "I trust you and I want you to stay with me because I don't know what I would do if I ever lost you."*

*She smiled at that. It seemed to be the right thing to say.*

*She goes to kiss me and her smell, never changing after all those years, comes rushing toward me like the tall wave of calming water that I've always meant it to be. It comes swirling, building, as large as a dream, about to come into me. Everything about the word "calm" becomes this moment. I don't care where we are, I don't care where we ever wind up, she comes in to give me herself in a precious abandon and I wonder how I could ever even be mad at her, or why I would want her to be upset. She was right. Women haunt, men only can live with it. It's a battle of wits, and I will lose, I will lose and have her in me for the rest of my life, and she comes into kiss me, and I accept it, because I know nothing else, I never want to know anything else, I just want all of this and her lips connect to mine and the smell is enough to take me to my grave, but I would be ok with it, because it would be the most alive I will ever feel.*

*She melts into my arms. She becomes one with me. She is my flesh and we are together, we will traverse these widened spaces, we will go one with footpaths already written, we will meet and we will create, we begin to stack light next to piles of undefeatable blackness. We fall to the floor of the group study room. We twitch, mad with desire.*

*We have begun our collapse as humans, we now begin our days as animals. We choose to do this. And it is a beautiful choice. We are adapting new styles way beyond our previous understanding. She tears my shirt off, but not before I close the blinds to the room, turn off the lights, lock the door, put a chair up against it, no one will break these barriers, we are invisible and invincible, we fuck for hours in that room, long after everyone has gone back home to each other, to sit and stare at their walls and wonder why, and wonder why, and wonder why*

A sound from outside jolts me awake. A car horn, someone screaming. Maybe something whispering into the morning of this day. I don't know. For all I know, it was her voice, speaking to me, trying to get me to collapse with her more. I try to go back to it, to finish it, because I wind up doing something again that I am not proud of. I try to go back to it. I'm close. I'm on the edge of understanding something. I'm on the edge of love, the line of love, one that fits, one that will fit and flow into me perfectly, but I fail.

I don't remember the rest of it and it's possible that I choose not to, because I don't know if anything was ever learned from it. Well, I learned one thing from it, I learned what her body felt like against mine in an awkward yet exciting space, but that does not change what has happened with me and her. It still has the same ending. Things were fine for like a week or so after that, maybe longer, but we went right back into the cycle, and nothing ever changed. I guess we went into the kind of acceptance where we walked on eggshells, unable to speak for fear of messing the whole flow of things, and she would get mad about dumb things, and I would get frustrated at her lack of understanding reality, but we made fantastic lovers still, and when things are going well on that front, there's not really much you can do. So we slept on nails with the perfect amount of caution, and did all those things carefully, like kiss, share, and breathe. We had become parents like hers, we had become parents like mine before they died, we became every conflicted duo that held hands before us.

I walk back into the bedroom and begin to dress. It's beginning to rain. Winter, our enemy. The dirty snow underneath our feet, the dark gray limitless cloth up above - the coldness, the fear of not finding a warm glove or a fire to sit by. I feel that she is thinking that too, for we both loved and hated winter at the same time. It gave us reason to be close. It didn't give us reasons to fight. I go back to a bright image of her stirring on our couch, underneath a heavy knit blanket, at the sound of a crackling log I just placed into the stove. The embers immediately died and the sparks flew, my skin began to turn red, and she woke up, fluttering her eyes. Full of love. I would turn and she would beckon me back to the couch. I close my eyes. I walk towards her and again...

I know what I did. And I have to fix it.

I made a decision based on fear by leaving her. I was afraid, simply, for connection. I had become paralyzed with the thought that she would become close to me that my death would mean her death, and I would not be able to live with her. If I were to leave, she would live - it made sense in my head, at the time. So I ran. I became something that I wasn't - someone who gave up. And it's because of that stray thought, a dumb thought, that all of this began. Because I couldn't open my mouth. Because I could not trust her to just beckon me back to sleep whenever I had a moment like this. I could not love her for a brief second, and so I left. I could not have her stop me on such a little thing.

I leaned against the wall, looking at my hands. These were not the hands of a man. And I began to flex them, make fists, count the hairs, ready to break the knuckle in half with my teeth, giving myself pain in order to live. I saw that these were the same hands that made her love me. I saw that finally, I was not living for just myself. I was living for another person. And for me to make such a horrible decision would have done nothing to help her. I brought her down. I let her down, and she got her revenge by haunting me, by almost kissing me, by kissing me, by sitting in our house and watching me leave, like a child.

Our house. She had made it a home. And I walked out of it.

I guess it's time now to really stop saying evil things about her. This isn't really a story anymore. It's almost more like a joke. There's nothing to really learn from this. It's just me talking about the girl that I love, the girl that I will always be with no matter what, the girl that I will always want to dream about, and here I am, saying things that could be half true or half false, based purely on anger instead of fact. It's a disturbing chain of events for a human being to go through when he can sit back through these flashbacks and find reasons to love the girl and then a minute later find reasons to hate the girl. Although I'm sure in the comfort of our own home - scratch that, our home - she's probably doing the exact same thing, which she has every right to do. I can only wonder how she chooses to word for word tell her story - put them in her order to make her side seem more significant. And see, that right there, that gives me hope and faith that somewhere in my body there's a reason for me to go back and I should take advantage of it. I can only imagine if she thinks the same thing about me. I'm still in love with her thoughts and I'm in love with my thoughts about her. I've told you enough bad things. I've been telling you the good things and the more I go into the story the more that I see that I rely on my memory then my anger. It's because my memory of her is what is more important.

Anger is temporary.

Love, a moment - that's something people want to keep.

The anger is subjective, you don't believe maybe half of it, I'm unreliable. I'm just a person that you barely know, a person that you unfortunately met. And here I come telling you horrible things about your life when I don't even know you, when you need to embrace what you have and have your perfect memories stay far away from my own, so they can never meet and become dirty. I can tell you what it was like sleeping with her. I could tell you what it was like camping with her. I can't tell you what it was like on a rainy afternoon, much like this one, the kind of day that you don't even want to move. It's the kind of day were the only move you make is the move you make towards her to kiss her and you make it count. You make it last. You make it the only thing worth living for. And I remember those days far too well - it's because it's one of those days now that makes you feel nostalgic as hell and all you can do is think. She is absolutely correct - she haunted me, and as you can see, she did a very damn good job of it. When I see her again, I will tell her that and I'll laugh if she remembers it, if she doesn't, I'll show her what I wrote. She needs to know what kind of impact she has. Maybe it's time to right the wrong, stop hiding. After seeing her yesterday, I knew that I made the biggest mistake of my life.

I sat down at the edge of the bed towards the window, looking at the rain fall on top of the snow. One mess after another. I couldn't move. All I could do was go in my head and think of the many ways I could have killed myself to save face. And I didn't go through with any of them. To go back to her now would take so much work, so much effort, I wondered if it was an effort at all. But then I slapped myself in the face as hard as I could. And again. And again. I made a fist and I punched myself in the leg. I took a finger and I put it back as far as I could in my throat. I gagged and the tears that came to my eyes, I wiped them off and I swallowed them back inside. I went mad, briefly, and it was to feel the same emotion that I had when I first met her. And it slowly started coming back. The indifference was beginning to fade. I went through as much pain as I could until I had to stop and catch my breath. The rain was not changing. The city outside still moved. They did not know the research I went through to make this story a story they might read. I was a sacrifice. They'd never know it, but she would one day, and I knew now what this has all been about.

It's about doing the right thing. It's about keeping what you have and making it work. If you love someone, if you want to have them, then do everything you can to keep it. Don't let them leave. I let her leave, I made myself leave, all of what love is about I mocked and tossed aside. And I can't forget all that, but it's time to remove the scar and let the skin heal. It's time to move forward. Never again would I ever do that to myself. I want to call her but I know she is sleeping. I know she isn't moving. I know she would not want to hear my voice. But I thought the hell with it. It's time to go back.

I began to pack my things. I grabbed all that I had brought, which wasn't much. I shoved everything I could in every bag I could find. I went mad again. I went into the bathroom and wanted to break the mirror for having been so stupid. I went into the shower and I kicked the faucets until they bent. I cursed myself for having spent so much of my parent's inheritance on this shit place when it could have been used for our future kid's college fund. I made so many shitty decisions that it's amazing if I ever made a good one again. But I knew I was now. I was coming back to her.

I started talking to her out loud as I moved around the room at a frantic pace. I won't tell you what I said. But it was enough to make me cry. It was enough to blind me and make me sit down in the middle of the floor, beating my hands on the ground. I hope she didn't leave. I hope she was there, drunkenly passed out but safe. I hope she didn't sleep with anyone else. I hoped she was still pure. I hope that we were able to start again. I want to go back to that college town with her, then, and retrace all our steps. I want to show her every word I wrote here and show her that I can share, that we are able to share things, secrets, and still be in love and independent and beautiful and young. I want to be able to say, I can stop the bad things. We can do this all over. We can move, we can walk. We can run together.

I made a much bigger mess of this apartment that I had intended. I opened the window and I let the rain come in, sideways, powerful wind burning its way inside, soaking all the furniture, ruining every last spot of it. I laughed as every last thing was left for the first unlucky asshole that came to rent out the place. I took this manuscript and I placed it in a paper bag - the only thing I had left to take - and I took one last look at what I had called this home away from her. And let me say one thing - it was shit. And I can't believe that I would ever want to come here. I watched the rain stream, surge, pour straight in for a few more minutes, then I pulled my cell phone out of my pocket.

I dialed our home number. I knew she would pick up on that - the ringer was the most annoying kind in the world.

Nothing.

I tried again. Nothing.

I laughed. The cell phone. I should have just done that first. I began to prepare the speech in my head - that I'm coming back, that it's all going to be wonderful again - and then I heard as my heart sunk so deep into the floor:

*"We're sorry, but this number is out of service. Thank you."*

I stared at it for a minute, then tried it again.

There was no way this could be real. No. It was just a flashback. Or something. I wasn't losing my hand. I started laughing again. I redialed.

*"We're sorry, but this number is out of service. Thank you."*

Fuck no. I took the battery out and I put it back in. I was sweating profusely despite the cold. I sung foreign songs in my head until it powered back on. No messages, full service. Ok, maybe a tower went down or something. Let's do this again.

*"We're sorry, but this number is out of service. Thank you."*

She had made her move. She made the last way to haunt me a wild one. I laughed again but then I realized that it was more tears than anything. I couldn't move. I put the phone back in my pocket, the mechanic voice so unlike hers, telling me the fate I gave myself. I think the rain and the room and the silence had a good laugh at that for a while. I could only stand as I heard the voice, the one voice I never expected, tell me again, that I was fucked. Both of them, at once, burning, writing in their own back story, wanting to give their own sort of love, knowing full well that theirs may have been better than mine.

part

five

Her car was gone.

I pulled up to the front of the house, for the second time in mere hours, and could only stare in the cold day at what lay ahead. I checked my watch - it wasn't even nine in the morning. And it was Sunday. Where could she have gone? What was she doing? Wasn't she drunk only just a little while ago?

I gingerly carried my stuff in the rain and dodged the snow. I looked up and down the street and saw nothing but an abyss, empty buildings laughing at me, off in their own winter dreams. I stood there, briefly, taking it all in. My hands froze to the bag handles, rough, calloused, but getting more of the pain that they needed in order to recognize the help that they would soon get. I went to walk forward and I slipped on some ice, but I regain my footing, got steady, and walked up to the front door. The locks weren't changed. All seemed to be the same. But I had a terrible, terrible feeling in my gut. I hope it wasn't what I was thinking. But I knew that she wasn't that kind of person.

But what if I taught her that, too?

I tried to open the door but it was locked. I put my stuff down to fumble for the key, but couldn't find it. I cursed and ran back to the car and looked everywhere, but I could not find it. Now, when I needed it more than ever, and it was perfect irony, a scene out of a movie, the movie that I'm creating for everyone to see. I remembered where the spare was kept and I ran out of the car, through the snow, around the side of the house, and under a gigantic fake rock that we kept next to the rose bushes. But the rock was gone, a hole was there, but nothing there for me to take. I cursed louder and I kicked the ground. Snow flew up and it reminded me of childhood. What I wouldn't give to be there now. Standing there with my parents, again. So far away from love and age. I shook my head free from the webs and debated how the hell I was going to get into my own house. She was really doing it this time. Outsmarting me. It is a war after all.

I wiped the freezing rain from my face and ran to the back of the house. All we had there was a small porch with a cement base and two lawn chairs, both fallen over, acting as wreckage, victims of the storm. I picked them both up and reset them, although a gust of wind knocked them back over and I continued on the frantic search. The back door was locked. All of the windows were shut tight. So I gritted my teeth and cursed myself for taking such a drastic step, but it was the only thing I could have done. You would have done it, too, if you were desperate enough, if you had wanted it bad enough. I picked up my stuff and I kicked the front door as hard as I could. It didn't budge. I kicked it again. Wood began to crack and I just kept rearing back and kicking, wound up and punched, kicked, punched, and then finally, I gave a shoulder block and the door fell into the foyer, me on top of it.

I landed hard on my side, my face hitting the wood. I immediately felt blood and I brought a cold hand to my face which made it worse. Wind and snow and rain blew in like an explosion and coated me quicker than I could blink. I cursed myself for what I had done and I struggled to get up. I picked the door up, struggled with it, and knew I wouldn't be able to fix it right with the proper tools, so I made a makeshift barrier by propping it up in the doorway and holding it there with a chair on the inside and a bureau from the living room on the front step. I had to laugh but at the same time, I was just shaking my head. Blood ran down my face and mixed with some flakes of snow and it made for an interesting taste. I felt a new sense of energy and I began to walk through the place with mad intent.

I shouted her name.

It was as if I was talking to myself.

Nothing, from what I could see, was moved. Everything was the same as it was when I was over last night. The living room had the same aura of tragedy. A beautiful girl drinking wine, attempting to read a book and watch TV, forgetting about her man. Seeing something snowy on the channel, seeing a couple in black and white, thinking to herself, what do they talk about when they talk about love? Not wondering or caring what her skin felt like, or her hair, because it didn't matter - she wasn't his anymore. It was like she disappeared. I hoped to God she wasn't dead. I wouldn't be able to handle it. I looked a little closer down at the DVD player. She must have been using it last night before I came over - a timer showed the familiar red letters and numbers. I pressed the open button and the slot spit out the disc, and I saw what she had been watching - the movie that I told her about in the diner about the old couple. I sat down on the floor and found the box nearby. There it was. She must had bought it in my absence, in an effort to get closer to my shadow. I put the box back sadly and closed it back up. I didn't want to know what part she was at. It would only hurt.

I looked back at the couch. More things of hers that she had kept near her, things I never noticed the first time around. A nail file. I saw an apartment listing book. I winched when I saw she had dog-eared certain pages. She was intending to at least abandon the house. Which I guess she had every right to, but still. I sat down on the couch and grabbed a tissue from a nearby box to wipe the blood off my face. It wasn't a lot, but it would leave a scar. I shivered from the wind outside coming inside, and I got up to move. I walked over to the fireplace. I might as well start a fire to warm up the house, so when she would ever show up, we could have maybe our makeup conversation a little more romantic. I opened up the gates and I was floored by the smell.

Instead of firewood and kindling, I saw old clothes I left behind. Shirts I haven't worn in years. Ripped pants. Socks, underwear. A leather jacket. And they had been doused in gasoline.

Where she had gotten the gas, I didn't know, but I took the nearby poker and I moved the pile around a little and it was more of the same. She was going to stay warm with the things that made my body warm once, and she would sit by the chair and not think of the fumes, and probably go to sleep thinking she was doing something good for herself. I closed up the gates and wiped the oil off my fingers with a little bit of melted snow from my clothes.

The clues were starting to become obvious. She had been prepared to rid this house of me, and at the same time, she was struggling to keep it the same for my return. We were both so conflicted. If only we had talked.

I made it into the kitchen and I kept calling her name, telling her to come out and settle everything for once and for all. No sense in playing roles anymore. It had been freezing in here, as well, so I went to plug in a little space heater we kept underneath the kitchen table to keep our feet warm while we ate, but as I looked down at the plug, I noticed that the prongs had been bent, unusable. I dropped the cord to the floor and only sighed.

What else had she done?

I picked up the home phone that sat in its cradle on the counter by our kitchen sink. No dial tone. I looked at the cradle and noticed that she had snipped the cord. Jesus Christ.

Why would she do that?

I looked into the refrigerator. There was barely anything in it for a meal.

The freezer was empty except for the ice cube tray.

I rifled through all the cabinets where we kept the dry food. That was all still there, but I noticed that she had pinpricked little holes into everything she could, making everything stale.

I opened the pantry and saw that she had peeled all the labels off of every single can, so that you couldn't tell what was what. You would just have to open it up and see. I laughed sadly. She was losing her mind. Why did I think this was a fucking game?

What had I done?

I opened up the cabinet where we kept all the plates. They were all stacked neatly, except for one. When I went to fix it, I noticed that she had written on it with black permanent marker. I pulled it from the pile gingerly and saw that, very delicately in beautiful script, she wrote: "Day One." I took a few out and saw that they too had been written on. "Day Three", "Day Six", "Day Thirteen". She had stopped after twenty. What had she done? I looked at the cups. The glass cups I saw that she drank them with lipstick on, as her lips remained permanent on them, like a piece of art. The plastic cups had been written on with the same thing - day this, day that. Confused, I let them crash to the ground.

I looked at the silverware. She had wrapped tape around them and wrote the same - day this, day that. She had made a weird routine only she could understand.

The bowls were untouched.

The coffee mugs were all left unscathed, except for my favorite one, my college alumni mug. She had broken the handle off and wrote on it, in the same black marker presumably, "free to a good home".

I started to tear up. I knew I caused all of this. It was all my fault.

I left the kitchen and I looked into the mini bathroom we kept on the first floor for guests only. Here I knew this would be the worst of it, and it was.

She had taken blue painter's tape and made a tic tac toe board shape out of it on the mirror. No letters were played. I looked into it and saw my face divided into squares, and realized it had been done perfectly, to include the eyes in the top two, the nose in the middle, and the mouth taking up the bottom. I could only stare. She was probably putting her face through some sort of system, in order to make sense of something. The sink wasn't touched, but all of the little things like the toothbrush and soap were all thrown away in the trash can, bag full to the top. I looked into the toilet and there was no water - she had emptied the tank. All I could do was just shake my head, but the biggest shot was when I turned and saw what was in the tub.

She had filled it up halfway with water, and in there, lay my wedding tuxedo.

It floated peacefully in the cold water, material ruined I was sure, white not even white anymore, the black being blacker than anything. I kneeled down and put my hand right where the tie would go. She had tied it nice and tight, choking me. Giving me no air. Giving me my bed to lie in. I leaned over the edge to take it out and hang it somewhere to dry, but I knew that it was pointless. She had done it for a reason and it was too late to do anything but respect it. I looked down at myself and knew that this was one early grave, with more to come. Blood dripped off my face into the water and I knew that was a proper sendoff. I quietly left the bathroom. That damage had been done.

I walked back to the front of the house and was glad the door was still holding tight. I picked up my stuff and walked up to the second floor, afraid of what I was going to find.

Slowly, with every step, I felt more and more defeated and anxious at the same time. I didn't know what I was going to find it, and I certainly didn't want to see any more horrors, but I knew that I had to, because that's what culmination means. It means that you have to put up with everything when you get to the ending. You have no choice but to absorb it, to accept it, to let it become you. I was no longer angry, I was no longer cocky, I was no longer anything than I ever was. I was a stranger in some place. Maybe someday they would find me breathing somewhere, with a new story to tell. Because I was slowly shedding this life. Dying. Waiting for another grave, one that would fit. One that could house such a lonely soul, such an idiotic man, such a man that has no balls or passion, and she would put the dirt in such a way that it would cover my face first. I would thank her for it, should I ever see her again.

I made it to the top of the steps. I should have went back down.

Up here is where our hearts are. It's the bed they sleep in. And I didn't want to see what she could have done to the real home inside the home, but I saw it, and this is how it went.

I walked into the spare bedroom to the right where we said one day it would be our kid's room. We promised we would get it cleaned up, we promised we would buy all the furniture and set it and build and paint it before she was even pregnant. We said we would be the best parents ever, and I was looking forward to it. But I'm glad, that because of how I turned out to be, that we would not be having a child. I could not father a son or a daughter knowing I made their mother into the kind of person she was. I did not want to say it happened to her parents and then it happened to us and then it would happen to them. I saved whoever was meant to come the indignity of having to live with us two, and although someday I want to be able to fix myself to the point where I can see a little version of me living, so I could teach it the right way to grow up and treat people. I would want to do that, but I can see she wanted to do this her own way.

The room had been painted bright blue. She had expected a boy in this fever dream. Crudely painted baseballs, basketballs, and footballs littered the walls, spaced very nicely. On the ceiling were little sticky glow in the dark figures of things - stars, animals, numbers. She had a brown dresser that would fit a little child's wardrobe perfectly, plenty of room for the little socks, the little pants, the little shirts. She had a little plastic multi-colored desk in the corner, with a lamp nearby, and on the table was a coloring book with a fresh box of crayons. Following the circle, she had a little playpen with a new box of building blocks, the price tag still visible in the one corner. Also, in the pen, she had arranged, with thought I'm sure, a few animals - a bear with a missing button-eye, a tiger with its sticking out, a red squid with googly eyes and many tentacles. Past that was the bed. Intricately tucked in, no sheets hanging out, a red and yellow comforter pulled right up to a lily white pillow. And right next to where I stood in the doorway was the closet, opened up, and fully stocked with jackets, extra blankets, other things that a little boy might want. In the middle of the room was just a notebook with a few words written down on the sheet.

I walked with baby steps to it. I knelt down and wiped the blood off my face so I wouldn't stain this grave. I looked at it.

And there, it had the name of our son. She had decided to make him a junior.

I wept.

She had designed this down to the last detail, and it wrecked me. If she were to return to kill me, it would be useless, because I was already dead.

The last dream I had, one that I made sure she would never touch, she had mangled, and she had done it well. I could not fault her. I had it coming.

I sat for a while and looked at my son's room. I'm sure she had visions while she did this room, that I would come back, like a soldier from war, like a businessman on a trip. She would be painting or rearranging clothes and he would be running a train across the carpet. Here comes the train, he would say. That's very good, she would say. She would ask my son if he was hungry, if he wanted any apples. Then the front door would open. She would have a mouth wide open with excitement and she would ask my son if that was me. He would run, he would trip over something, skin his elbows, keep going, and he would stand at the top of the steps with his mother, and there I would be, untainted, untouched, no blood, no anything other than what I was when I first met his mother, and I would take him and swing him in my arms -

*- much like my dad did when he came back from the -*

I shook my head. No memories right now.

*- and Mom would be so happy because they had so much to -*

\    I shook my head again, harder. I wiped my face. I slapped myself and the wound stung. I couldn't do this. Not now.

I set the notebook back down and I looked at the stuffed animals. Happy with their grins and no brains. Never close to any kind of truth much like me. They're just there to be friends. They're not meant to do anything other than love.

Why couldn't have I been like that?

The tears came harder when I opened up the drawers to the dresser. Every little shirt you could imagine. Folded perfectly. No wrinkles. My son's clothes. He would have been set for life.

I couldn't take any more of it. I just couldn't see what it was going to be like had I never left. I shut the door. I made sure it was shut tight. I didn't want anything getting in that room. I was bad enough.

I went to the bathroom right next to the spare bedroom to wash my face. I tried turning on the light to see but nothing happened. I assumed all the bulbs were burned out, but as I took out my cell phone to see, I noticed all the bulbs were taken out. Why, I had no idea. A sick joke, perhaps. But that's all it is now, at this point. You see that, right? Destruction and broken hearts, it's a perfect way to start the day. I moved my cell phone around to shine a light bright enough to see if everything was normal and it looked like it was. Except for one thing.

I walked to the tub and saw the same ritual had been done.

She had taken her wedding dress - one of impeccable exquisiteness, words could not express how angelic she looked in it - and she had drowned it the same way she had done for me. It lay dead and suspended in the water, begging I'm sure, for some sort of savior to pull her out of the sea and return her to home. The necklace and the bracelet had been placed in there gingerly, at the same place her neck and wrist would be, for the full effect. The veil as well. All flooded and awash with tears and misfortune and sad endings. I put the cell phone down on the counter and I set it to keep the light on as long as it could. I knelt down, wiping away the blood one more time, and clasped my hands on the lip of the tub, as if I was praying or proposing again, staring into the hole that she had created. There she was, her body, laying there. Her soft spirit, one who has toppled mountains and watch me struggle with inconsequential bullshit, a essence that only knew how to love me and nothing else, one that was an orchestra of sound in even the most noisy room, dead at my feet. I remember the day like it was yesterday - your wedding day, you just never forget - and I remember speaking to her the best way I knew how, I held her hand, her bracelet grazing my thumb, her eyes broad and spacious, showing futures I had no idea were in existence -

*- I had wanted to get married at night and she wanted to get married by a fountain -*

I shook my head. I can't.

*- she had been yelling at the caterer and I was being pushed around so she wouldn't see me and everyone was telling me I was done as a free man -*

Stop.

*- and we had danced to Everlasting Light by The*

-

The tears fell into the water on her veil.

*- and as I kissed her I told her that I knew I was going to marry her ever since -*

I started talking to her again. Whispering her name, then shouting. Asking for forgiveness. I just wanted the world to end with her by my side, whether she hated me or not. I wanted things to be peaceful again.

*- her saying as we made love that night, that it was ok to share now, we had no secrets anymore, our flesh was together, we had the same blood now and that there was nothing to be afraid of, nothing at all, darling, nothing at all to even worry about -*

I stood up and pulled the wedding dress out of the bathtub. My cell phone light had since gone out, but I didn't care. Not one bit. I stood in the dark and I did what I had to do. I hugged it close to me and I was drenched. But I didn't give a shit. I wondered what would happen if the neighbors saw me. I tried to get that night back in my head. I wanted to feel it. But I couldn't do it. I stopped. What was the point? She wanted it this way. I have to respect it, I have to, it's what she wanted, it's her way of coping, it's her house, it's her vision of love.

*- as we danced, she was repeating a poem she heard, something about love as the rain that makes the wheel of life turn, something about the green grass of somewhere being as powerful as a kiss in the morning to*

*start the day, and I held her close, and thumbed the outside of her hand, feeling it all bore into me, feeling it all scar into me, and she told me that her father really did like me after all, and that her mother was going to try to start talking to her father again, and maybe we could have dinner with them someday and that she was sorry my parents were dead -*

I threw the dress back into the tub. It splashed violently and water flooded over the edge onto the floor. I didn't care. It was all material things now. The feelings were gone and the memories didn't have the same luster. I fished the bracelet and the necklace out and I laid them back into the original position they were in as best as I could. Sleep tight, my darling, I whispered. Maybe one day we can have that dance again. It was the best dance in my entire life. I walked out of the bathroom. I left it all sit there, like the mess it was.

The final room was our bedroom. The king of kings, the box of magic. Where we protected each other from harm. Where we kept each other safe from strange people and Mother Nature and the coldness of an unstable, immature universe. Where we read books -

*"- maybe one day, babe, I'll be in a bookstore and I'll see your books on the shelf and I'll buy one and tell everybody that I'm married to this man -"*

-and watched movies-

*"-how can you sit there and watch this shit, I'll never know -"*

-and discussed having kids -

*"-so if it's a boy, we can either call it Junior, or we can go with something different if you like, and if it's a girl, I got it all picked out, I'm stuck between four names-"*

-and worried about the economy -

*"-I didn't think we would have pinch pennies this year, but let's not get ourselves anything for Christmas, ok-"*

-and had problems with sex -

*"-it's ok, babe, tonight just wasn't our night -"*

-and dreamed of having other, newer, more exciting lives.

*"-I always dreamed of learning an instrument, maybe going on the road, kinda being like Aimee Mann but being a lot more talented, you know, like someone maybe like that girl who was that big indie star for a while in the 90's...what was her name -"*

I opened the door and thanked God she wasn't dead in her sleep.

Everything was the same as last night except her. The bed was a mess. Everything else was a war zone. She would have wanted it this way. I took my coat off and let it fall to the floor. There was no point. She wasn't home. She was out in the rain without a cell phone looking for me, maybe. Looking for a new home. Someone to hold her, someone to caress her. Someone to listen to her theories. Maybe she woke up and hit the road like she wanted. Perhaps she wanted to leave this all behind, maybe this nonlife was just not good enough anymore. I looked around the room. If she had left, she had taken nothing. She had just went off into the horizon, searching, hands wide open, asking for anything other than what she had.

I dropped my bags on the ground as well. No sense in carrying it around. Maybe I should just lay down and wait. There's nothing else to do. Go and lay in bed and-

*"-but there's nothing else to say, so what's the point of talking to you - "*

Think about all the times we shared.

*" -that's why it hurts to talk to you. it hurts to talk to you no matter what time of day. I want to trust myself to be open with you, but I'm so used to playing other characters around you that it's hard to become me...I know, I'm talking in circles. I really am. But I'm drunk and you won't remember any of this in the morning, you won't remember the girl that's speaking it. I mean...you'll*

*wake up and remember this...and you'll be hearing the words, but you won't be listening...you'll just be lying there and you won't even take a moment to realize that the person who's pouring all of this out of her body has no soul left...so it's just this body that's speaking, but not doing much of anything else...and you know what's sad? I won't know when to turn away either - "*

Think about all the times I shared with my beautiful wife who poured me coffee.

*" -it's not that hard to speak, you know, you just open your mouth and try to say whatever comes to your mind - "*

Think about all the stories I wrote to her when I was half-drunk and she was only half-caring about the world in front of her. Think about all the stories she tried to write in an attempt to be exactly like me.

*" -she laid there in silence allowing the shadows to envelope her in lies and loneliness. She cried in the sheet with the window opened but no one knew she was there, the hands glided and grasped the cold bed and remembered the warmth it once held. The silent night cried for her and the man fell into the shadows as she wished the night to remember the fast forward motion her mind once held. She replays it day and night, and yet the memories held nothing she could grasp. The movie of her*

*mind continued without her, and she stayed where she was, cold on the sheets, grasping and breathing like she did before...what do you think of that ending, babe -"*

I pushed all the thoughts away as best as I could, although I know it would be pointless. They would just come right back in a few minutes. I pushed all the junk off the bed - clothes, whatever else - and let it fall to the floor. I crawled into my old side of the bed and lay on my side, watching the rain fall to its death outside.

I thought maybe I would get answers by coming over here. Obviously I just get more questions. When did she choose to drown the tuxedo, the wedding dress? Why would she prick holes in the food? Why would she cancel her cell phone in only a matter of hours? Where is she now? Where did she go?

Who is she with?

I thought I would have been the hero, the knight in saving grace. But I'm a character in a game, soon to die of static. Soon to run out of lives. Soon to run out of parts of which to move and fend off demons that have my name and number. And I could feel the beginning of that coming too, resorting to things way beyond my control, in order to help control the new feelings I was sure to get once all of this is over. When I find out she's dead or with another man. I can see myself writing about it now, in a diner somewhere, or at someone's house when I have nowhere else to live -

*"and parts of him vanished when it came to him she was not returning, not coming back, not ever speaking, not even one more warm breath on his skin, not even a warning or a promise of what lay beyond.*

*and he was presented and introduced to other people as a walking tragedy, as a lover who has lost, a loose chain with now a staggering weight of a love dragging, choking, drilling into him as night and day no longer mattered, no longer looked different.*

*and midnight became the worst time for him as his door closed shut, never to open for her, as his room - this only room now that would ever mean anything in his life - was now his space, his spot, his shelter. it had everything and nothing all at the same time, a cold bed, open books with no answers, and places for his mind to run into, pictures of her when she was beautiful instead of gone, and to think, they were so young - so fucking young."*

I wake back up, out of the quick daydream. I think I hear a noise. But I hear nothing. It's my mind losing, breaking down, running wild, imagining her in a body that will not come back. I know this now. Coming here was useless. I knew, just by looking at the things she did, that she wasn't coming back. What does she have to come back to? There's no hope, there's no nothing. Just a lot of walls that laugh and scream and want to hug you but they have no arms, and all they know is how to speak what you last said, to make you replay it forever, as a signal, a tone, a calling for the rest of your existence. It was her, throwing me a last line, a rope. Maybe she was up above me, and I'm on the raft, like that dream I had of her, and she's screaming at me just to die and move on, and I just won't get it, because in the end, I just don't understand a goddamn fucking thing about life.

I roll over to look at her side of the bed. Almost immediately, I project an image of her naked body, her hair loosely falling over her back in front of my face, freshly washed. Softly snoring into the night. And I hold her hand, my other arm tucked behind her neck, kissing the back of her head tenderly in a chance that it'll give her better dreams. Trying my best to transfer love from my heart to mine, and once I asked her if it worked, and she mumbled something and just went back to bed. I smile at the memory. Looking straight ahead, I see her bureau. Full of most of her things. The chair she sat at. Her hairbrush. Her makeup, her lotion, her jewelry. Many times did I see her standing or sitting there, getting herself ready for me, getting herself prepared for whatever adventure was to come. And I thought about all the times I've seen here there, and it began to get clear, clearer than any other vision that I've had all day, and I sit up to stare and I know what's going to happen before I even do it. I'm going to bring myself to this moment that I didn't want to do. But now, looking at her things, imagining her, the smell, the feeling of her skin after she was done, everything about her...

I sat up. I undid my belt and zipper, pulled down my pants. And I stared at her bureau. I was starting to say to myself, don't do this. This won't help. This won't make anything better. This will only make it worse. Stop. You don't want to go down this path. But I do. I do because there is nothing I can do to stop myself because I am an animal who prefers suffering and who likes to see these things destruct and die in front of him. I do because she turns me on and there is nothing I can do to escape the fate. It has been like this ever since I left and this is the closest I am to her so I have no choice but to submit. And I start.

I'm staring at her things because I know they're hers and it helps. I can see her doing it all. I can see her getting ready for her wedding day. Sitting somewhere, getting ready to share her life with me. And she's nervous, she's scared, she has her sister and her mother by her side, trying to give her good words of faith, and she's holding a smile tight, afraid that if she drops it she won't be able to bandage it back up and re-use it. And she's putting lipstick on - wait, no, she didn't wear lipstick at the wedding - and she's brushing her hair, her long, thin, gorgeous hair that she took a long time to prepare for me and her mother is whispering things to her very quietly so no one else hears, things about life and what she could have done differently - stop, that doesn't have to do with this, go back to her - so I imagine her putting the necklace on, the white gold gracing her porcelain, frail skin, the cold of it giving her a little shiver, and then she puts the bracelet on, very carefully, possibly an heirloom and it makes her more elegant and dignified and then she puts on the final touches of her makeup - her mascara, her eyeliner, very carefully, one stroke at a time she gets herself ready to be the most stunning woman on the planet and she does it all for me, all for me, and I don't know what to think other than I just don't appreciate it, I'm on the other side of the building, thinking about everything else but love because people are telling me that their experience was different, their wedding was something entirely different -

  - I stop to take a breath -

  - and I keep going, looking at her things, and I remember her coming down the aisle, one of the true happier moments of my life, seeing her for the first time, finally, all ready, all set to be bequeathed to me, and she's walking very slowly, her father walking her, hand on the small of her back, and she doesn't know what to do at first, she's almost envisioning something else, like she missed a step or something's out of place and I'm afraid she wants to run but she sees me and keeps going, I was her motivation to do something with her life, and finally, she gets dropped off at the altar and I see her smile at me and I go to tell her she is beautiful but she made me promise not to say anything so I just mouth it and she mouths something back and I hold her hands and they are incredible, and I keep going I keep going and I want to just finish this and go back to bed but I see her things and it keeps my brain going on infinite play and the priest says some words, I'm not entirely sure what they are or what they mean and she looks at me and holds this smile like it's a child, and I want to say to her, it's ok, you don't have to hold it the entire time, it's ok to let it drop once in a while, but she holds it, because she is a woman and she is stronger than me and she is one hundred percent correct and the memories flood, and I remember the stars breaking through above us and it had threatened to rain but it decided at the last minute to go in the other direction and the priest goes on about love and I wish I knew what he was saying but I am so taken aback by her beauty that I am paralyzed, I have nowhere to run, I cannot write anymore, I am destined to be another crappy husband in a suburban town with a white picket fence and all this other shit -

-and I stop and I breathe. I'm nowhere near close. I'm getting myself caught up with thoughts. I can't rely solely on emotions anymore it seems. It's a terrible thing to admit it, but sometimes, you just are not a man, and you can't do what's expected of you. But I don't want to stop. It'll be the last time I'm ever in this room. When I go back to sleep, and if she's not back by the time I wake up, I'll leave. There's no reason to stay. It saddens me to say it, but this probably is the last reason, and once I'm done, that's it -

-so I continue and she's reading her vows she wrote to me and it's the best thing she could ever write. She tells me, in one very well written paragraph, how she will honor me until my dying day and even days after that, she will obey my words and she will take care of me, she will hold my pain for me when I have only so much room for it, she will stand by my side as I make ill-advised decisions on our future, she will watch as I fuck our kid up and tell him things he will not like, she will stand there and bite her knuckle as I worry about money and get rejection letter after rejection letter, she will lay with me in bed as all of our dreams will be lit on fire again and again and again and then I snap out of it when she smiles because she is getting to the best part about how I am lucky to have her because she is a bright, intelligent, beautiful woman and I helped her realize it a long time ago, and that it'll be a wonderful thing to be able to share a life with me, the only life we have, and you can tell the crowd wants to clap and cheer and go wild but it is time for me to say what I have to say and at the one time where I'm expected to talk, I simply cannot do it, I cannot do it for my lips are dead, my well-rehearsed speech has fallen by the wayside and I am gone, further gone than any other shadow that ever walked into a room, and she's waiting, and her beauty starts to falter, her mask starts to slip, and I'm a blank page getting blanker, a novel being erased, until I stumble and I talk about how love is a right, not a privilege, and she smiles carefully, and I am simply awestruck by the fact that such a gorgeous woman wants to be by my side, and right as the sun starts to drop behind the mountains, I can hear the nearby ocean crash and sway, and I say something that I think is very nice, about how the sea is eternal and so is our trust, how it waves and crashes and breaks but it is still intact, much like the human spirit, and she has no choice but to tear up and I go to kiss her but I hold back because it is not the time, and she mouths something to me, and I'm suddenly afraid that everyone is judging opinions, but now, and this is the rush, the moment of love, where the priest is done his spiel and he says you may now kiss the bride and I do I do I finally do and the love I finally have is only physical and not emotional and what the fuck did I get myself into and we kiss and they cheer and her hands find their way on my cheeks and I smell her perfume and I feel her hair and I am so close to finding happiness that when she pulls away I pull her right back in and the audience cheers louder and I can feel her arms I can feel her body on me in that white wedding dress and just before she breaks away -

-I'm coming very close to finishing, I can feel it -

-I feel her whisper to me -

*-now, we have all the time in the world, you and me, to love and be together -*

-And I start responding now in real life because I did not when she said that to me and I shout her name as I keep going, I want her to hear me wherever she is, and I beg, I plead, I just want her to come back, I want her to come back and see me, I want her to come back and hold me and tell me it's alright because I just don't want to do this anymore, I don't want to do this to myself anymore, I want to be a part of her again, just come back and love me so I don't have to resort to this shit anymore and she leads me by the hand -

*-our first steps as husband and wife -*

-And I feel like I'm ready to die and I feel the blood on my face and I'm so close to finishing and as we walk down the aisle touching each other she squeezes my hand and that is enough for the climax and I scream her name as loud as I can as I let myself go all over my hand, my lap, our sheets as the memories starts to fade out like a move, and I am left panting, breathing heavy and hard, trying to stop my heart from bursting out of its cage, and I am spent, I am tired, I can't move, I just lay there, with one hand still on it, the other hand clutching the headboard, breathing, a mess, trying to remember my wife on her wedding day and I cannot go to photos and simply look but I have to do it this way and I begin to cry, mutter her name, think of the ways I can make it up to her, think of the things I should have said differently, wished she never haunted me, thinking up of different ways to try to contact her, and I'm about ready to pass out. I might have actually for a few seconds, because the next part happened so quick I barely had time to react to it.

I hear a loud bang. A crash. A loud noise. It's her. It's her voice. I don't move. I realize I'm fucked for a second.

She's here.

How does she know I'm here?

My car.

All the shit in the house, she knows, I've been here, she can smell me.

I just don't move. I didn't clean up but I am frozen by fear. She's going to come up here. Where has she been?

I hear her shout my name and I say nothing. The broken front door is a dead giveaway. I should have been a little more careful. So much for being subtle.

I hear her rustle around looking for me, calling me, as I start to move quietly to clean myself up. I do not want her to see me like this. I should have planned this a hell of a lot better. But it's too late. Another grave. Another spot for my head to lay.

She's at the bottom of the stairs.

She calls my name as loud as she can, but she knows it, she can feel it, she knows exactly where I am and she wins, she can't wait to tell me, she cannot wait to see me in this spot, wondering where the hell she was. She wants the confusion and she wants the pain and she set me up perfectly and she loves every minute of it, she loves me for it.

She runs up the stairs.

No sense in moving. I'm done.

I take a deep breath, I lick my lips. I'm totally dehydrated.

She stops, looks in the spare bedroom, and mutters something to herself.

She's checking up on her - our, sorry - son. Everything's in order so she leaves.

She runs into the bathroom and she almost slips because of the water from the wedding dress. She shouts my name. I can't answer. I really don't want to answer. I just want to surprise her now. There isn't much time.

I try to think of a good way to start the conversation, but I can't think of anything even remotely good. Silence, again, is golden.

She stood outside the bedroom door, whispered my name.

I don't know if I said anything because she came in slowly.

And she saw me.

I saw her. It looked like she had been dressed for church. That's probably where she was, there's no other logical explanation for it. At this point, there isn't a logical explanation to anything. She showed no signs of being hung-over, lovesick, tired, anything. She looked young. She looked nineteen years old again, coming up to me in the diner and talking to me about books. She looked like she was ready to be proposed to.

And I had nothing to say. I sat there and stared at her.

She looked at me and cocked her head, almost unsure of what to say or do. She saw my mess. She saw me guilty as charged.

I looked at her for a few seconds, closed my eyes, and started to say something before she shook her head at me, like I had been caught committing a very embarrassing crime. Like I was a kid. Like I was ready to be punished.

I started to cry but I held it back.

She dropped her purse and balled up her fists.

I almost began to plead.

She took a deep breath.

Very slowly, I wiped my hand off with my sleeve and zipped my pants back up, still half-erect, still ready. I didn't even want to reflect on it as a possibility, but the way she was standing there, I halfway considered it. It may have been the right thing to do, oddly enough.

She started to move.

And I did too.

And that was pretty much the end of it.

I barely had time to get off the bed before she came at me, screaming. I didn't want to hit her but if I had to, I had to. She had come here to kill me. I was sure of it. But I soon found out that wasn't it, it wasn't it at all.

She managed to get on top of me first, and she was trying to kiss me. But this was not gentle. It was hard, very rough. She tried to pin my shoulders down but I wasn't going for it and she dug her nails into my skin. I yelled but she kept going, trying to pin me down, trying to kiss me. She found my lips and she began to suck, like she wanted to rip my tongue out with her teeth, but she was trying to just tongue me, and my mouth had stayed closed.

She said to come on, to kiss her.

I tried to wrestle away from her but I didn't realize how strong she really was.

I spun out of the way and she was on the bottom but she quick turned and grabbed me by the arm, pulling me back in. She scratched me while doing it and I yelled.

I told her this wasn't right.

She called me a nasty name.

I told her to stop and she wouldn't listen.

She moved back in to kiss me and pull me back down. She told me that if I didn't like it so much, to do something about it, and she called me another nasty name. I had to get her to stop, through any means necessary.

Her hands met mine in this test of strength battle and I pinned her down to the bed, her eyes covered by her hair, her body ravaged with shaking, her lips trying to reach mine.

I told her that this wasn't there, this was another woman.

She dug her nails into my palms with a little bit of glee, a little bit of malice and she assured me that this was her now, and this is how she wanted to be, and that she wanted as bad as anything. And I was the only one who could give it to her.

Once again, I fell back down and she clamored on top of me, her lips finding my neck. She sucked as hard as she could, trying to make a mark.

I laid there for a second and realized her hands were trying to pull down my pants, trying to get me back out and into her.

I tried to wrestle away. I didn't want to strike her but I had to do something to get her off me. This just wasn't right. It wasn't right at all. I didn't want it to end like this. That's not how I planned our day to go.

I quick wrapped my arms around her and I pushed her away but she hung on to my waist and we rolled off the bed and onto the floor. My back had hit the drawers on her bureau and the knobs dug into my spine. As I laid there for a second, catching my breath, she sat up and began to undo her blouse. Her breasts fell out in front of me and she let them dangle in front of my face, begging me, inviting me. She was murmuring something but I couldn't make out what it was. I probably didn't want to know.

I sat up, knocking her off. She lay on the ground panting for a minute, staring up at me.

I told her no.

She had eyes like loaded guns, ready to go off. Her naked chest danced in front of me.

I told her I was going to leave and let all this behind as a nightmare, that I was going to write it off and we were going to forget this ever happened. Her soft white skin teased me but I wanted to leave it behind with other pieces of myself, but she just wouldn't let me. She wanted the taste of love just one more time.

I went to step over her but she grabbed my ankle and pulled me in and I fell on my stomach and hit my face on the floor. She climbed back on top and she saw my wound on my face from earlier when I landed on the door.

She put her lips on it and kissed it, and then began to suck. It stung so I tried to push away but she held on, trying to get all the blood she could out of me. There was nothing creepy about it. It was sensual. She just wanted her husband back.

But I tried moving again and she held me down. Her lips found mine and we were kissing again, and she was kissing hard, harder than she ever kissed before, trying to get all of that passion back. Her hands once again were going for my pants and she started to pull them down further. I sat up and started to move up and found myself back on the bed, her on top of me. I pushed her away with my hands and she came right back down, trying to kiss.

She looked beautiful.

But this just wasn't the time.

I tried to stop her. I said her name.

But she wouldn't hear it.

Her hand found my penis, still only half hard, not really wanting to go down but unable to really do anything else, and she started to stroke for me, but very hard, very unaware of the power she had at the moment. I tried backing away but she held on and I pushed her away with my hand. She fell back and I squirmed away, off the bed and stood up, staring at her as she sat on her knees on the bed, panting, running a hand through her hair. She began to strip down to her underwear. I suddenly felt very scared.

We tried finding words but we could find none.

She got off the bed and made a lunge for me and I didn't move in time and we knocked over a nightstand and a lamp crashed and the bulb burst and something went into my other cheek, a shard of something. I was bleeding from both sides and she seemed to be excited by that and she lay on top, trying to kiss me again. I was losing the verge to fight. I was thinking of caving in, but she started to try to masturbate me again, really hard, and I got mad. So I unfortunately did something I wasn't very proud of.

I slapped her. I had never hit a woman before, and never wanted to. I saw what that did to my parents. It is never a good thing.

It was not a good slap or a hard slap, but it was enough to knock her back. Clearly she wasn't expecting it and she got off me and stood up, leaned against the wall, her head buried away from me into her hair.

I got up and felt the shard digging into my cheek. I pulled it out and threw it on the ground. At this point, my pants had fallen around my ankles, so I just took them and my shoes off so I wouldn't trip. I was naked, which is what she wanted.

She began to cry as she stood there, holding her face.

I started talking soft to her. Anything I could think of, I said.

She turned around and I saw a dark face that not even my dreams could have conjured up. She was red, her dignity crushed. Even topless in the barely lit room, she was still stunning.

I said that I was sorry.

She started to sob harder but she held out a hand, not wanting me to get closer.

I told her I did not want to do that, that she was too beautiful to hit.

She nodded. She was naked except for her underwear. She looked like she had never left that little town. She looked like she never wanted anything to do with me.

I asked her to believe me, that I didn't want to hurt her, that I never meant to run and hide, that I never meant life to be a game.

She spit in my face.

I told her not to do it.

She tried to mumble a response. I'm sure she had a good many in her head, but none that she wanted to say out loud. She did not trust her tongue to tell me these words. She would rather stay silent to me than try to patch things up. She just wanted action.

I told her to listen to me.

She asked me what I was doing back here, in our bed. She asked me what it was that got me to go. She asked me a million questions at once through her crazy tears.

I told her I was there to get her back. I didn't know how else to say it. She would just have to believe it. I started to tell her I had all these wild dreams and flashbacks about the two of us and that it all meant something and I realized how women haunt men and I didn't want to be haunted anymore, I wanted to be together.

She showed me her face after I spoke. I winced. I bruised her. I didn't think I hit her that hard. I don't know my own strength. I don't know a lot of things, about myself or her or anything at all anymore. Holding her face in her hands, she proclaimed that I didn't want her back as a person or anything, but just a plaything, and that was our new role so we might as well embrace that instead of each other.

I tried to tell her that she was wrong, that it wasn't the case. I wanted to hold her body again as we slept and tried again.

Tried what?

I said one word, marriage.

She laughed.

I asked her why else would I be here, what other reason could I have to be in our house again after all these years.

She whispered that it was because I came back to make fun of her, and to rub it in her face that I was happier without her.

I stated to tell her that I was not happy at all.

She spit at me.

I tried again.

One more time.

I told her very quietly not to do that again, and that I was not happy at all, and that I wanted her to make me happy again...

And then she slapped me.

And then I grabbed her out of anger and I threw her down onto the bed.

At first, she resisted. I tried pinning her down and she fought and I was screaming at her that I wish I never met her, that I wish I never had anything to do with her, how could she do half the things she did to me, and she was screaming over me, wishing me dead, asking me how I could come back, asking why I even left at all, and we had just started yelling loud enough to wake up the whole world.

She dug her nails into my chest so hard that she drew blood.

And I tried to get her to stop but I couldn't.

She wrapped her legs around me and she started to squeeze to shut me up.

And I tried to wiggle out but I couldn't do it, and she begged me to just go inside her and be done with it but I couldn't even move.

She started going on about how she wanted to fuck every guy she saw for the last couple of years but she didn't because she loved me. But she still wanted to just to make me jealous because women haunt men and that's all they really ever do.

So she did remember. I was proud of her.

And I told her to stop, I couldn't breathe.

And she said, good, that's exactly what I want.

And I told her to stop before I did something I would regret.

She let go with her legs but her nails still dug into my chest and I yelled at her to knock it off, that this wasn't how I wanted to end this.

She began to say something about my parents, and instead of hitting her again, I kissed her, just to shut her up.

And she took it.

And all the feelings started to go away.

I started to lose what I had just gained for her - respect. She was losing whatever it was she was trying to get out of me - hope. There was no sense left in appealing to good nature. Simply put, this was the last war we were going to have. I went with it.

I kissed her rougher than she had kissed me.

Her hands traveled all over my body, scratching, pulling, pushing, bringing me in, pushing me away.

The screams quieted, both her and mine.

I stayed on top of her, sucking her breasts while she played with me, trying to get me fully hard. It wasn't working.

She begged, she pleaded.

She talked to me like she did the first couple times we ever had sex, come on, she would say, you can do this for me, baby. Just forget about everything, like it's the very first time, we're getting to know each other all again, I want to feel connected, things like that.

And I couldn't do it. I kept saying I was trying.

So she fumbled on top of me, and I wasn't cooperating, so she pinned me down again and she went to kiss the wound on my cheek but I told her not to and she did anyway.

This is not what I saw in her on that wedding day.

And she started to try to talk dirty to me but it wasn't working and she gave up.

And she tried to fit me in her despite me not being ready and she stopped and took a deep breath and sucked on her teeth and tried doing some other things.

And I told her that it wasn't going to work and she got mad and called me some names until I pushed off her and told her that was it, I wasn't going to stay, I was going to leave.

Then she grabbed me and tried to bring me back and I wrestled with her, saying I wasn't, until she scratched my bare back and I howled and I turned around to push her back down but she stopped and instead of kissing me rough, she kissed me nice and gentle.

I took it.

All of a sudden, the tide turned and we began to kiss softly, like a new married couple would, or even an old couple that had nothing else to prove.

And soothingly, tenderly, as best as she knew how, she brought me down onto the bed, on top of her, on top of her sheets, the ones we used so many times before.

And she begged me to remember the motions, the curves of her body.

To think about what I was thinking about earlier before she came in.

And memories flooded and dreams got bigger and I slowly began to find her body like I wanted to, but half-heartedly, the other half of me wishing that I could just get done and leave, but the other half saying that this is the last night, just take it before you leave, just take it for the moment that it is and quit worrying about the specifics.

So we began our old routine.

She kissed like a time bomb. Again and again on my lips. The touch of her hand on my chest felt softer than a series of clouds absorbing into me; so sweet was the sensuality of her attention to me.

I decided to open up. I reached into myself further and I melted from what I might unearth onto this beauty. In my tongue, I collected water for her thirst and passed it onto her. Her skin went through transformations in my slowly-weakening grip; it came to me in handfuls, then finger rakes along the slender back, in light strokes all over, then palm to breast, as I traded with her millions of beads of sweat.

We were undergoing intentions of sin and of no patience. We were unraveling feminine and masculine twine.

We were throwing away reality.

She flicked her wrist upwards. I sat up. We faced each other.

I felt inclined to reach for her hair but with a firm clasp, she grabbed my hand, placed it with the other, and held onto both of my wrists at once. With the other hand, she clawed at my back until my head rolled back in ecstasy.

She continued now on the chest until ribbons of faint red appeared. She loved the pain she was causing me and she even moaned at it as I sucked my teeth and let air flow into the fresh scratches.

After this, she let go and she lay down on the bed, stomach down.

But I still couldn't let myself get fully ready.

And I knew why.

But I couldn't tell her.

She started to get mad again.

She wanted to know why I couldn't get hard.

I began to tell her that I wasn't ready for this and I wasn't feeling very well and we can just leave now and forget all about this.

And she came at me again and I pinned her down.

But instead of kissing her again, I thought about what she represented instead of who she really was. I looked down and saw that she was just a mere shade of who she was when I saw her. And that me bringing myself to climax was not her but just the idea of her. And that her name, her actual body, it didn't actually really mean a thing. And I'm sure she thought the same of me. There was no sense in saving her anymore, because it wasn't her I wanted to save, it was my idea of love.

She pleaded some more about why can't we do this.

And I forgot her name.

I treated her just like any other woman.

I started kissing her again and I started to get hard and she liked that.

She begged me to go in her and I wouldn't and she started to get mad but then she stopped again and she just let whatever it was happen that I wanted to do.

My skin was bright red and fresh blood and my neck was full of her kisses and she said that her cheek hurt when I slapped her.

I said I was sorry and I kissed it.

She grabbed my penis again really hard and I told her not to.

She said just to get in me and get it over with, she was very tired, and I told her I was too.

All of these things swirled around me and I could not stop it. I had reached a fever dream and was unable to know what direction to take to get out of it.

I asked why her she had canceled her cell phone but she wouldn't answer me.

We kept kissing and I was slowly immersing myself back into her.

She called me another man's name.

I stopped and looked at her, asked her what she said.

She called me that name again. I won't say it out loud.

The most anger I ever felt in my whole life hit me like a train. I felt like I wanted to die. I didn't know what to do but I pinned her down as hard as I could. And I was slowly getting ready to go in her.

She did it again.

The anger swelled and so did I.

That's not really how I planned on doing this.

And she was begging me to just end it and that she wanted it and that she dreamed about it for three years now, that I would come back and give her the son that she wanted.

I said I was sorry for making her crazy.

She said that it wasn't me that made her crazy, that it was the world, and that she did everything in her power to stop being influenced by it, and that it wasn't my fault. She talked very smoothly, very lovingly, choosing her words based on their size instead of their meaning. She was trying to go back into how it used to be.

I told her it wouldn't work that way anymore, and I called her a different name.

She grit her teeth.

I did it again.

I leaned down and whispered in her ear, another name of another person.

She tried to move and I held her down.

I was ready to go inside of her.

But she told me she didn't want to call each other names. Could we just end this normally?

I told her no, we had gone too far now, and I started to talking to her like I never met her.

She began to cry but she brought me in and I got on top of her and slowly, I fit into her like the last piece of the puzzle.

We both moaned in delight but I knew it was to be short lived.

She started moving her hips even though I wasn't moving yet.

She was asking me where I had been living.

I told her that it was just a place, some place, nowhere big.

And she told me to move, to give her everything she's been dreaming about for three years ever since I left, that she never could imagine getting this from anyone else.

So we started and I thought about the twists and turns I should have took to save her instead of the ones I did take to save myself. It was stupid thinking I was the only person that ever had feelings, that I wasn't the only one who needed help. She had been here the entire time. I tried telling her this but all she kept saying was give me your hips, give me your hips, I want it, I need it.

And I tried shaking my head free from the cobwebs, I couldn't get to it, but it felt good to her, and that's all that matters.

I had a brief flash of that night of our wedding, where I took her back to the bedroom and we did the exact same thing, but now, this was just a retelling, and it just wasn't the same. But it was necessary, and that's why humans fail. We look at our memories, decide they're not good enough, and we recreate them, and we make them a lot worse than they really were.

She says the other man's anger to make me care more.

I do, briefly.

I say the other woman's name and she finds a way to get me deeper in her.

I told her I'm sorry about the bruise.

She says she's sorry, she didn't mean to hurt me so hard.

She didn't want to attack me.

I told her I didn't want to hit her.

She asks me to give it to her.

I told her that I would be done soon, that I feel it coming.

*- I remember the last time we did this before I left, it honesty was the most passionless thing I had ever done in my life, and I'm sure she was thinking of someone else during it, but I didn't care, I was so defeated, I just want it done so I could move on with my life. She didn't see it that way. She saw it as me being with her forever, conjoining, being the same. How wrong she turned out to be on that one. It was a shame that such a beautiful girl wound up being so sad, and a man with good intentions wound up doing nothing but no good for all his life.*

She told me that she wanted to feel me, she needed to feel it, she needed to feel something again in her life.

I told her that it wasn't going to be great, that it wasn't going to be much, I had nothing to give her anymore.

She alternated in saying my name and the other man's name.

I leaned in and whispered her name.

And she started to cry. She was happy.

I said it again, like the refrain from a prayer. As gently as I could.

Her eyes opened and they were wet and they saw me and she was so young, way too damn beautiful to be wrecked.

I closed my eyes and I just wanted to hear the detached sound of love fill the room.

She kept moaning, she was close, she said.

I told her I was too, I told her to  make the memory last, it would make a great flashback someday.

She dug her nails into my sides.

I let the blood trickle down onto her fingers.

I had to give her something of mine.

She told me that she wanted nothing more to feel close to me again, to feel all of my words and my sadness and my anger, that it was enough to give her hope for the future.

I said nothing and I told her that I was going to come.

She told me no, not yet, she wanted to go at the same time.

I told her that these things happen and we don't always get what we want. And my eyes started to go fuzzy and I felt the rush coming.

She told me to hold back.

I looked over at the window to see the rain. I didn't want to see her face as I did this.

She felt it come and she told me she loved me and she screamed my name, not the other man's name, and I smiled. She had got it right this time.

I gave her every last piece I had stored up. I continued to watch the rain.

It was a beautiful thing.

She made her noises and she made her motions and she was spent, too, maybe she had gone and I just didn't see it or notice it but I couldn't make eye contact with my wife. She wasn't my wife anymore. She was all that I ever knew about love and that didn't make her anything else than what she was. An image.

I tried to catch my breath but I hate breathing air but I had to in order to lay down with her, be able to hold her.

She laid there, gasping for air, wanting to run.

But I was on top of her and I held her down.

She kept whispering my name, she didn't want me to pull out, to stay in for a few minutes, just not to move, keep it there.

I nodded, seeing that my body had marks all over it like a map. I saw them and counted them in the darkened room. All was quiet. The snow and the winter and the loneliness had made this a place to go to remain unattached from all forms of life, except us two, who had no idea what we were going to do from this point on, except remember, or forget, or a combination of the two concepts.

I know our words were short and maybe not meaningful enough, or our memories not strong enough to do anything other than just give you something to look at, but it's just life, you can find a story elsewhere that can do more for you, maybe, if you're lucky enough, but this happened to be my story, my part of love that I was willing to share, even though I couldn't even share it with her. It just happened to work out that way. I'm fucked up enough to admit that. Maybe it's better having strangers see this instead of ones who really, truly care. But if this story did something to you, then I guess I made my point. I shouldn't have looked at love as indifferently as I did.

And if you do, do something to get you out of it. No one deserves to look at love like that. I was in the wrong. I just want people to be able to love who they love, and not get caught up in the bullshit.

I couldn't watch her as her body went through her climax. It was the last part of our ritual, I had forgot that she liked to lay there and feel it all, relive it quickly. It gave her some hope.

I watched the raindrops kiss the snow.

I flexed my muscles one more time, gave her one last thrust after she was done, she always liked that, and she moaned my name in delight.

But I was too sad to care.

We had no color to our bodies. We were just cold, gray people trying to move in mid-morning rooms. We were like our parents.

All she kept saying was my name and not to pull out.

But I did because I was tired and I didn't want to play out the scene anymore. There was nothing else to do. As I pulled out, she squealed and then moaned sadly, whispered my name, told me that she loved me.

I told her I loved her too.

I walked into the bathroom and cleaned myself up in the dark. I saw the wedding dress laying in the bathtub.

I had nothing else to care about anymore. It was a sight that unfortunately won't ever change, not even in my dreams.

I walked back into the bedroom and she lay there, on her side, curled up, staring at her bureau. Normally I would ask if she was ok, and she would nod or mumble something, and I would roll over and go to sleep. But I went over to the window and saw the snow and the rain. Two different things, but still, the same. I guess that's what we were. Even though we were so far gone in our own darkness, we still had met up long enough to do something, and when time goes, we melt, just like other people we knew.

It was really a shame.

I saw a hell of a future between us.

I closed the blinds that gave us the only light in the room. I looked over the destroyed floor, the ruined bed. It was a great puzzle. I'm sure she had her pieces set. She would fix it later. If I stayed to help, so be it. If not, then there was no great loss.

I crawled into bed on my side.

She reached for my hand and I gave it to her and I smelled her hair and I smelled her skin and everything was exactly the same. She had never changed. Just me. And that was pretty much the end of our battle. We had fought, we had clawed, we had become animals, and I knew that we would have moments like that, at some point in our life, but when you get down to it, you just don't see things like that when you first meet and when you're in public. But behind closed doors, all bets are off. They just are. Not everyone is like this. Just us. And it's how the cards are dealt. There's nothing weird about it.

Some people are just unlucky.

My eyes closed and she said she loved me.

I didn't answer right away.

I must have fallen asleep because she had turned over, began to stare at me, and she kissed me on the nose. I woke up and I saw my wife's face.

I'll never forget this part as long as I live.

She looked at me dead in my tired eyes and said, simply, like she did so many years ago: "We'll sleep for now. You can hold me like you want. You've had your final time. But when you wake up, I never want you to come back here again. If I ever see you again, I'll do a lot worse. This is over. But just enjoy it for now. It'll be the last time you touch me. I'll make sure of it." And she started to kiss me again but she stopped, and she held back two tears, and she rolled back over, back into the same position we always slept in, holding my hands, and within seconds, she was asleep.

I laid there with my eyes open, thinking about what she had said.

She had finally made it easy for me.

*

## Acknowledgements

First, I'd like to thank Mark Pogodzinski of No Frills Buffalo for the incredible opportunity he's given me in publishing this book. Here's to literature, my friend.

Second, to my family. I know I hide all this writing from you, and you probably wonder if it'll ever come to anything. But perhaps one day we'll see just exactly where it goes. Much love.

Third, but not last, my friends. I would love to acknowledge you all, but time and space may not be on my side for that one. Well, here it goes: Aubrey Magargal, Caren Bean, Toni Waltman, Seth Lawrence, Kim Dahms, Dawn-Santos Martinez, Maranda Stewart, Bobby Foxx, Charles O'Blosser - all of you and many more, thank you. Truly. From the bottom of my heart, I give you the limit of my respect and gratitude. I'll try to pay you all back one d

www.ingramcontent.com/pod-product-compliance
Lightning Source LLC
Chambersburg PA
CBHW062113170626
46813CB00002B/433